April
and May

Also by Jane Peart

April and May

Jane Peart

Fleming H. Revell
A Division of Baker Book House Co
Grand Rapids, Michigan 49516

Published by Fleming H. Revell
a division of Baker Book House Company
P.O. Box 6287, Grand Rapids, MI 49516-6287

Printed in the United States of America

Library of Congress Cataloging-in-Publication Data

Peart, Jane.
   April and May / Jane Peart.
      p. cm.—(Orphan train west)
   Summary: When her parents and aunt die, May Chandler discovers that she was adopted and that she has a sister somewhere, and May is determined to find her.
   ISBN 0-8007-5724-6 (pbk.)
   [1. Orphans—Fiction. 2. Adoption—Fiction. 3. Sisters—Fiction.]
I. Title.
PZ7.P32335 Ap 2000
[Fic]—dc21   00-040288

Scripture is from the King James Version of the Bible.

For current information about all releases from Baker Book House, visit our web site:

            http://www.bakerbooks.com

Boston, 1895

The huge railroad depot was cold and drafty, the acrid smell of coal oil strong. The station echoed with the hiss of steam engines, the metallic clanging of wheels on steel tracks, the rattling of luggage carts. December wind sent soot and cinders whirling along the cement platform where a line of children stood waiting to board the Orphan Train.

Winona Roth, a worker from the city's Child Welfare Department, tapped the arm of Clara Donohue, the woman in charge of the orphans. She raised her voice to be heard over the noise. "Couldn't you reconsider?"

Miss Donohue looked up from the clipboard she held and shook her head. "No, that's impossible."

"But," Winona persisted, "the mother of these two little girls asked that they remain together."

"She should have thought of that before she gave them up for adoption," Miss Donohue answered sharply, then frowned and asked, "Are they twins?"

"No, but—"

Miss Donohue's face took on a pained expression. "The answer is no. As I told you, we simply can't handle all these individual requests. We have twenty other children to place, you know." She shook her head. "It's out of the question. Placing two children in the same family would be too big a burden. We have trouble enough finding families who will take just one child."

Winona made one more try. "Couldn't you make an exception?"

"How old are they?"

"Three and four."

"Oh, well, then they're old enough to adjust. They'll be fine. And in any case, an agent makes yearly visits to check on the children, and if she finds they're unhappy or ill-treated, other arrangements can be made then. I'm sure once those two are settled in new homes they'll quickly forget each other and their mother too, for that matter."

With that Miss Donohue ended the conversation and walked away to the other end of the platform.

That seemed a harsh judgment indeed to Winona. She turned to look at the two little girls for whom she was pleading. The smaller of the two clung to the hand of the other one.

They were certainly an appealing pair. Round, rosy-cheeked faces, wide hazel eyes, ash-brown curls under their ruffled bonnets. With a pang of guilt, Winona remembered her assurances to the young woman who had brought the children to the agency. She had been hardly more than a girl herself. Slim as a wand, almost too thin, with a sweet pretty face and large haunted eyes.

Maybe she should have fibbed, Winona thought guiltily. Maybe she should have said they were twins. They looked enough alike to be twins. Maybe then Miss Donohue might have relented and agreed to find a couple willing to take them both. Well, it was too late now. They were beginning to board the children onto the train.

Winona blinked back tears. She had often been warned about becoming emotionally involved in the cases she handled. All these children's stories were tragic. She could only hope and pray that their endings would be happier, that the children would all find loving homes, parents who would care for them. As the whistle blew and the train began to move slowly down the track, she whispered a special prayer for the two little sisters who had so touched her heart.

The train that had left Boston five days before trundled over the trestle, chugged down the tracks, then pulled to a stop at the yellow frame station in Emeryville, Arkansas.

On this chilly December morning, a crowd of people, including the mayor and members of the city council, ministers of several of the town's churches, as well as the simply curious, thronged the platform. The editor of the local newspaper, along with his best reporter and photographer, was there. This was a big story for the small community. Tomorrow's edition would feature it with banner headlines and pictures of the children.

Two couples awaited the arrival of the Orphan Train with special anticipation. Both couples, childless after several years of marriage, hoped to find among these homeless waifs a child to call their own.

Ned and Peg Barstow had driven all the way from Penfield, a small rural township about thirty miles from Emeryville. Not able to have a child of her own, Peg was desperate to adopt. Ned traveled as a salesman for a farm equipment company, and she was often alone and lonely. A little girl would be company and someone she could lavish with love and attention. They were accompanied by Ned's mother, Agnes Beiderbaum, who strongly disapproved of their plans to adopt. "It's like buying a pig in a poke," she declared over and over, but her protests fell on deaf ears.

Walt and Annie Chandler had a more sympathetic companion in Annie's sister, Wilma Rogers, who had come with them to the station that day. Wilma, too, would have loved to adopt one of the children, but her husband, Joe, was an invalid confined to a wheelchair, and she had all she could do taking care of him.

As the children came off the train and lined up on the platform, Annie clutched her husband's arm. "Oh, Walt, see those two dear little girls in pink? The little one looks so sweet. She's the one I want."

"You're sure?"

"Yes. Let's take her before anyone else does. Hurry, go on," she urged. "We can sign the papers later."

As it turned out, it wasn't as easy as that. When Walt bent to pick her up, the child resisted and began to cry. When he finally managed to lift her, she held out her arms to the other little girl, screaming, "Cissy! Cissy!" over his shoulder as he carried her to Annie.

"Here, take her. I'll see to the paperwork." Walt gave the sobbing child to Annie, who turned to Wilma in panic. "Oh, what shall I do?"

"It will be all right," Wilma replied as she patted the little girl's back. "She's just scared. Everything's so new. She's probably worn out from the long train ride," Wilma said soothingly as they went to the buggy.

"But how can I get her to stop crying?" Annie sounded on the verge of tears herself.

"You'll be home soon and you can give her some cocoa and some of the cookies you baked."

Finally, Walt, flushed and out of breath, joined them. He climbed up into the buggy and turned to his wife. "Everything's taken care of. Let's get on home."

"I'll see you back at the house," Wilma told them. "As soon as I check on Joe I'll come right over and help you get her settled."

"Thanks, Wilma." Annie nodded gratefully. Having her competent sister next door was always a great help. On the short distance to their house, the child's choking sobs gradually became long, shaky breaths. Soon she was sleeping.

"I hope she'll be all right," Annie whispered anxiously to her husband.

"Don't worry," Walt reassured her. "Some of the other children were carrying on just as bad. It's a big change for all of them. Everything will work out just fine, you'll see. We've got our little girl." He looked over at Annie and smiled. "Happy?"

"Oh yes, Walt, I've never been so happy."

But when the buggy stopped in front of their house, the little girl woke up and the wailing started again. Her arms tightened almost in a strangle hold around Annie's neck, and her cries became terrified screams again.

In the cozy Chandler kitchen Annie sat down in the rocker and tried to comfort her. She was relieved when the back door opened and Wilma came in.

"I can't seem to get her to stop crying, Wilma. She keeps sobbing, 'Cissy, Cissy.'"

"That's probably her sister, the other little girl that was dressed just like her. A young couple took her, but they were having a terrible time with her too. She was kicking and yelling something awful. Didn't you see them?"

"No, I didn't see them. I was too preoccupied trying to get this little one calmed down. But Walt said something about it."

"Well, these children have been through a lot. That was a mighty long train ride for youngsters this age." Wilma touched the collar of the pink coat the little girl was still wearing. "May. Her name suits her, doesn't it?"

10

Little by little, with lots of coaxing, the sisters got May to sip some cocoa from a pretty cup and nibble a cookie. Then her eyelids began to droop and she leaned back on Annie's shoulder and soon fell asleep.

Meanwhile, back at the train station the scene that Wilma had described continued.

"No! No! I don't want to go home with you!" April yelled. Her little arms flayed, and she kicked out at the man trying to lift her, shrieking, "I want Mama, I want May!"

Ned Barstow gave his wife a helpless glance. Peg stood wringing her hands in distress, dismayed at the temper the child was displaying. They had just signed papers to keep her until she was eighteen. What if it was, as Ned's mother insisted, a mistake?

Peg thought of the small room that used to be her sewing room that she had fixed up with pretty new curtains and a pink bedspread for the little girl they both wanted, the child to make their life complete. During all the weeks of waiting for the Orphan Train to come, Peg had been so excited. Now, as she watched her husband struggle to control the angry little girl, Peg worried. What if it didn't work out? What if the child remained this unhappy?

The fact that Ma Beiderbaum was witnessing the scene made it that much worse. Peg glanced over at her. Ma's face was grim, the corners of her mouth turned down like a croquet wicket. Disapproval was written all over it. She didn't need to say a word, but that didn't stop her.

"Well, there's a temper for you!" She shook her head. "Mark my words, she's going to be a handful. I wouldn't put up with this for a minute." She wagged her finger at her son. "What that little rascal needs is a good spanking, Ned. She needs to know who's boss right from the start."

"Please, Ma," Peg protested gently. "Ned will handle it."

"Hmmph," Agnes said and stomped off toward their buggy. With much huffing and puffing she got in. There she sat with her heavy arms folded belligerently across her well-corseted bosom.

Finally, Ned cajoled April to come with them. He picked her up and carried her to the buggy with Peg trailing them.

"Whew!" he said with a chuckle, winking at Peg as they settled April between them in the front seat and started off. All the way home Peg kept feeding April lemon drops from the small bag she had brought with her, which seemed to keep the little girl quiet, if not happy, until they arrived at the Barstow house.

As soon as they got inside, April turned sullen. She plunked down on the floor, pressed her small mouth together, and scowled. If Peg hadn't been so upset about the little girl, she might have laughed. April's small face looked a lot like that of her mother-in-law. This was a far different homecoming than the happy one she had imagined.

Peg knelt down to the child's eye level and gently suggested that April might enjoy a warm bath to wash away the grime of the long train trip.

"We'll put some of my scented bath salts in the water. Wouldn't you like that, April?"

Grudgingly, the little girl nodded and went with Peg but refused to take her hand.

As Peg led the way upstairs, she heard her mother-in-law say, "Well, Ned, you've bought yourself a peck of trouble, if I know anything. A regular little scalawag. Spoiled to boot. You'll have nothing but misery with that youngun."

"Now, Ma, it'll just take time," was Ned's smooth reply. "She's just a frightened little child. She'll soon see we love her, and she'll do great. You'll see."

"Oh, Ned, you're an incurable optimist, always were and always will be."

"Well, it's better than always looking at the worst side of things, isn't it, Ma?" He laughed. "Besides, Peg wanted this little girl badly, so let's not spoil things for her, all right?"

"It's just too bad you didn't have children of your own—"

"Now, Ma, don't start. You know Peg has a heart condition, was never strong enough to have babies. Please, don't bring it up. It will only make her feel bad. And right now she's happy."

"Hmmph. And how long will that last with that wild little critter?"

Her mother-in-law's sharp retort made Peg wince, and she promised herself, We *will be happy, all of us. I'll see to it.*

2

Within weeks April settled into life with the Barstows. Little by little she responded to Peg's devotion
and Ned's jovial personality. Gradually, his teasing
coaxed smiles, then giggles, and then uproarious
laughter from the little girl. The atmosphere in the
small country house was always cheerful. Even
though Ned was sometimes gone for a week at a time
or longer, Peg gave April so much loving attention that
the child flourished.

April's memories of her real mother and baby sister
gradually grew dim. She began to call Peg "Mama,"
and as they were left alone much of the time, they grew
very close.

Peg had been a teacher before marrying Ned, and
she discovered that April was bright and a quick
learner. She taught April numbers and letters, and
together they read stories until soon April was able to
read for herself.

Among some of the happiest times were when "Daddy Ned" came home. His homecoming was always like a party. Peg cooked his favorite dishes, and April helped by frosting a cake or picking berries for a blackberry cobbler. Ned usually brought home surprises, often new records of popular songs.

One song he especially liked was "Peg O' My Heart." "Come on, Peg, my darlin'," he would call out before grabbing Peg around the waist and swinging her across the floor. They would dance all around the front room, out into the hall, and even into the kitchen, as April turned the handle on the Victrola, its large brass horn shaped like a morning glory. Then Peg would lean against the kitchen table, laughing and gasping for breath and saying over and over, "Oh, Ned!" Then Ned would turn around, pick up April, and dance around the house with her.

By the time April had lived with the Barstows for nearly three years, it seemed as though she had always lived with them.

April loved all the same things Peg did, especially gardening and handicrafts. Since the school in Emeryville was too far away for April to attend, as was the one in Penfield, Peg took over April's schooling. After lessons were finished in the morning, they worked in the garden, planting and weeding in the spring and summer, and in the fall tying back annuals and harvesting the vegetables.

When the weather turned cold, they spent enjoyable times together making dainty corsages and decorative bouquets from fabric flowers. Peg showed April how to fashion silk roses, velvet violets, and satin and lace ribbon into all sorts of creations. They also made book covers, slippers, and handkerchief cases for gifts and for the church bazaar their neighbor Mrs. Simmons always attended.

April's life with the Barstows was pleasant indeed—except for the times Grandma Beiderbaum came to visit. April always dreaded those. Peg explained that her mother-in-law lived alone and got lonesome. However, the day she left was always an especially happy one.

One of the things Peg and April did every day was walk down to the country road to get the mail from their rural route box. Mrs. Simmons, their neighbor, was usually there at the same time. When Peg drew out a letter from the batch and gasped, Mrs. Simmons asked in alarm, "Not bad news, I hope?"

"Oh no. It's just that—" Peg hesitated. "Ned's mother is coming for a visit next week."

April's heart sank. Things always changed when Ma was there. An air of tension surrounded the house like a tight wire ready to snap. Ned's mother never hid the fact that she thought April was a nuisance.

As they slowly walked back to the house April asked, "Why is her name different from ours, Mama?"

"Well, you see, Ned's *real* father died when Ned was just a baby, and his mother married another gentleman, Albert Beiderbaum," Peg explained as she folded the note and put it in her apron pocket.

"Oh." April paused. "Then where is Mr. Beiderbaum?"

Peg hesitated. "Well, I'm not really sure, April. He doesn't live with her anymore."

There was no other explanation, but April secretly didn't need one. She didn't blame Mr. Beiderbaum. Who would want to live with the crotchety old lady? Right away April felt guilty. She knew it would make Mama sad if she knew April had such ugly thoughts. She would try to make Mrs. Beiderbaum like her this time.

At the house Peg said, "We have a lot to do before she comes. I want everything to be nice and for Ma to have an enjoyable time with us. You will try to be sweet, won't you, dear?"

At April's downcast face, Peg gave her an impulsive hug. "I know Ma seems cross sometimes, but we have to remember she is old and probably lonely. Anyway, I want her to see what a darling little girl you really are. You will try extra hard while she's here, won't you?"

Above everything else, April wanted to please Mama and not do anything to upset her. This time Mrs. Beiderbaum would not find anything to complain about or scold her for. April would also try to think of something special to show that she was not "the awful mistake" Mrs. Beiderbaum declared her to be.

For the next three days April helped Peg as she got everything ready for their guest. They hung freshly washed and starched dotted-swiss curtains at the sparkling clean windows, put a new bedspread on the brass bed, with a bright afghan folded at the end.

Daddy Ned was going to meet his mother at the Cloverdale train station and bring her home when he returned from his day's round of business calls there.

Peg told April she would pick some flowers from the garden at the last minute, arrange them in one of her prettiest bowls, and place them on the table beside the bed.

Weary from all her exertion, Peg told April, "I'm going to take a little nap, sweetie, so I'll be all rested and refreshed when Ma arrives. Be a good girl and find something quiet to do while I'm resting."

I know, thought April, *it will save Mama the trouble if I get some flowers and put them in here for her!*

There were lots of pretty golden flowers blooming in the empty lot next door. She wouldn't take any flowers from Mama's garden, she decided; she might pick the wrong ones. Instead, she'd gather bunches of those bright yellow ones growing so profusely. The color would brighten up the spare bedroom that was shaded by the leafy branches of the big maple tree outside the window.

April wasted no time collecting the flowers for the surprise bouquet. Then she quietly opened the china cabinet in the dining room and got out one of the cut-glass crystal vases, filled it with water, and carefully carried it upstairs, tiptoeing past the bedroom where Peg was sleeping.

Worn out by all the rushing around she'd done the past few days, Peg slept deeply. When she awakened, she hurried downstairs, smoothing her hair back just as Ned's buggy came to a stop in front of the house.

"Welcome, Ma," Peg greeted her mother-in-law, who came puffing up the porch steps on Ned's arm.

She leaned forward to accept Peg's kiss on her cheek then immediately began complaining about her trip. "Hot, and dusty, and a lot of misbehaved children on the train. Then Ned was late meeting me, and I'm tuckered out and thirsty."

Peg listened sympathetically then suggested Ma go up to her room, freshen up, then come down for some cool lemonade.

Ignoring April's little curtsy she'd practiced with Peg and still grumbling, Mrs. Beiderbaum went heavily up the stairs.

Peg and Ned exchanged a look. Ned made a hopeless gesture with both hands, palms up, and Peg nodded. Just wait until Ma saw the vase of flowers, April thought happily, then she would feel better and be nicer.

However, the next thing the three standing in the downstairs hall heard was a screech followed by a series of loud sneezes. Mrs. Beiderbaum came to the top of the steps, her face blotched and red. She was shaking the bouquet April had put in her room. "Who put these hideous weeds in my room? Don't you know even the sight of these can bring on an attack of my hay fever. *Goldenrod,* for heaven's sake!"

Later, Peg tried to comfort the weeping April, who had fled to her bedroom to avoid Mrs. Beiderbaum's rage. "It wasn't your fault, darling. You couldn't have known."

"She hates me. She'll never forgive me now," sobbed April.

Even Peg couldn't deny this. She knew her mother-in-law too well.

This time Mrs. Beiderbaum cut short her visit, claiming that staying there made her asthma worse. The household breathed a sigh of relief. This had been one of Ma's worst visits. April was particularly glad to see her go. Mrs. Beiderbaum's steely gaze seemed to follow her everywhere, and she never lowered her voice when she made one of her disparaging remarks about "that little scamp."

Things soon settled back to normal for the Barstows—but not for long.

Emeryville, 1898

Clara Donohue, the agent for the Orphan Train Society, straightened the brim of her straw "boater" hat, touched the bow at the neck of her coffee-colored blouse, and shifted her folder more firmly under her arm before ringing the doorbell at 29 Maple Avenue. This was her third visit to the Chandlers since placing a little girl with them from the Orphan Train.

As she waited for someone to open the door, she glanced around at the wide porch with its white wicker furniture and hanging baskets of begonias. Indeed, this orphan had been fortunate, even if her adoptive parents were a bit older than most. She had been placed in such a comfortable home in a nice neighborhood. She just hoped the girl wasn't being pampered. Miss Donohue set her mouth in a straight line. Such treatment never boded well for an orphan when he or she grew up and had to face the real world. She fervently hoped that wouldn't be the case with little May.

Any further thoughts were interrupted by the door opening. "Oh, Miss Donohue!" Annie Chandler exclaimed, looking flustered. She nervously wiped her hands on her apron. "I wasn't expecting—"

Miss Donohue smiled faintly. "That's the point, Mrs. Chandler. The Orphan Train Society makes impromptu calls to see how everything is going in the homes where we place children."

"Of course, I remember. Do come in. May and I were just baking cookies—things are rather a mess—"

Miss Donohue stepped inside. "Well, we don't want things spruced up just for us, Mrs. Chandler. We want to see the ordinary, everyday way things are."

Just then a little, round face lightly dusted with flour peeked from behind the swinging door that led into the kitchen. "Who is it, Mama?"

"A friend, dear. You remember Miss Donohue, don't you? She visited us last year."

"How do you do, young lady?" Miss Donohue asked.

"Fine," May said as she bobbed a curtsy.

"Here, May, sweetie, take these cookies next door to Auntie Wilma and Uncle Joe. Tell Wilma I've got a visitor and ask if you can stay over there a little while."

After May went out the back door with a plate of fresh baked ginger cookies balanced carefully in both hands, Annie turned to Miss Donohue.

"I thought we could talk more freely without May here. You see, we haven't told her she's adopted."

Miss Donohue frowned. "Do you think that's wise? She'll have to find out some day, and it might be in a cruel way. Sad to say, there is a stigma attached to orphans, and it may come at a severe cost to her in later life."

"Oh, we know that, and we do intend to tell her when she's older. It's just that—"

Miss Donohue flipped open her folder and took out a questionnaire. She had other calls to make in the area, one in Penfield thirty miles away, for which she'd have to hire a horse and buggy. It was time to get down to business. "Well, I hope you won't regret your decision, Mrs. Chandler. Now, has May had the mumps or chicken pox?"

As Miss Donohue went through her list of questions, Annie happily answered no to all the negative ones. She was sure May was a happy, well-adjusted child in every way.

Miss Donohue seemed pleased as well and soon was on her way to her next visit.

As the hired horse plodded along the country road to Penfield, Clara Donohue noted the widely spaced houses. Used to the bustling, busy city of Boston, she found the stretches of open countryside and the houses set at a distance from one another quite depressing. With no close neighbors and no nearby children to play with, was April finding her life with the Barstows a lonely one?

To her amazement, the opposite was true. April was a lively, talkative seven-year-old who seemed eager to join in the conversation. Finally, Peg gently suggested that April go outside and gather a bouquet of flowers for their guest.

It was Miss Donohue who felt a trifle uneasy. She looked somewhat out of place in the Barstows' brightly decorated parlor. Evidence of Peg's creativity was everywhere—in the flowered curtains and slipcovers, the framed watercolors, the plump colorful pillows, and the vases of fresh flowers.

As Miss Donohue started on the list of required questions, Peg immediately launched into a recital of April's many qualities. "She is the most loving child, sweet tempered, always wants to help me with everything. Ned simply adores her and—"

"That is all fine and good, I'm sure, Mrs. Barstow, but there are some basic questions I need to ask you again," Miss Donohue interrupted, her pen poised above her questionnaire. "Such as church attendance. I assume you and Mr. Barstow go to church regularly and send April to Sunday school?"

Peg hesitated. Would Miss Donohue understand if she told the truth about their rather haphazard and infrequent church attendance? Would it somehow threaten their adoption of April? The fact was Ned was often away from home over the weekend, leaving them with no transportation. Their nearest neighbor, Mrs. Simmons, sometimes invited them to hear a special speaker or to attend a social at her church. But most of the time when she and April were home alone, they had a little church service of their own. They would pick flowers, say prayers of thanksgiving, and read Bible stories. It was difficult to explain, but those times had become very meaningful to both of them.

Miss Donohue accepted the explanation and went on to the next question, so Peg did not have to tell her that even when Ned was home, she often didn't feel well enough to go out. It was something she didn't like to talk about. She never complained, not even to Ned. She was happy and content to stay at home with her daughter.

A half hour later, Miss Donohue drove away, the bunch of wildflowers April had thrust at her laying on her lap. She was satisfied that the orphan placed with the Barstows was healthy and thriving. Just as she had predicted to that emotional social worker, Miss Roth, April and May were both doing just fine, in spite of being separated against their mother's wishes.

Emeryville, 1898

May had been looking forward all summer to the first day of kindergarten.

"You're going to love it, precious," Annie told her as May sat on the high kitchen stool trying not to wiggle while Annie combed her hair into ringlets. "You'll make friends and learn how to do all sorts of fun things. Paste and cut and color. Play games, sing songs."

As an only child, May was sometimes lonely. She longed for playmates like the children in the picture books Annie read to her. She didn't realize that the Chandlers were older than most parents and did not know people with children her age. At school, she would have lots of playmates.

Just as Annie buttoned May into her starched, ruffled pinafore, Aunt Wilma came in from next door.

"All ready to go, honey?" she asked May. "I have a little something for you." She pulled out a tiny handkerchief on which she had embroidered May's name and the date September 1898. "So you'll always remember your first day at school." She tucked the hanky into May's pocket and then cupped May's chubby little face in both hands. "Have a happy day, precious," Aunt Wilma said, kissing both of May's rosy cheeks. Over May's head Wilma looked at her sister with tear-bright eyes.

"These have been the happiest years of my life," Annie said as she smiled back.

They had been happy ones for May too. She was the center of the Chandlers' life as well as that of Wilma and Joe. It was unlikely she thought about her "Cissy" anymore. The past had faded into a loving present, surrounded by doting parents and an adoring aunt and uncle who lived next door.

As Annie predicted, May did love kindergarten. She found it every bit as fun as Annie had promised. She enjoyed everything about the routine—pledging allegiance to the flag, marching to the lively tunes Miss Wilson played on the piano, listening to stories, drawing and coloring with fat, wax crayons, drinking milk and eating graham crackers at snack time, walking home with her best friend, Miranda. May was carefree and happy, that is, until the day Betty Sue Jamison handed out invitations to her birthday party—to everyone except May. On the way home from school, Miranda explained, "Betty Sue's mother don't let her play with orphans. And you're an orphan."

"I am not!" May retorted indignantly. She did not know what the word meant. But it must be bad if it was why she had not been asked to the party. She ran the rest of the way home. Hot-cheeked and breathless, she burst into the kitchen. "Mama, Miranda says I'm an orphan. I'm not, am I? What is an orphan?"

Annie turned around from the stove where she was stirring apple butter. Her face drained of color. Her eyes widened in shock. She stared at May for a minute, then without answering she gathered May up and held her tight. She sat down in the rocker with May in her lap and rocked her for a long time. After a while she said, "Run next door, darling, and ask Auntie Wilma to come over. Tell her I need to talk to her and, oh yes, tell her we're having a party."

Uncle Joe was on the porch in his wheelchair whittling when May ran up the steps.

"Whoa there. What's your hurry, young lady?" He grinned at the little girl he adored. He had fashioned a wooden Noah's ark for her with dozens of intricately carved animals and was always adding to the menagerie. May paused to admire his hands shaping a giraffe. "Where's Aunt Wilma?"

"She's upstairs working on her scrapbook. Pasting in pictures she took at the Fourth of July picnic."

May went inside and, calling Aunt Wilma's name at every step, ran up the stairs.

"In here, honey," her aunt answered. May loved Aunt Wilma's room. There were so many interesting things to look at. She had a "whatnot" stand filled with the

31

china figurines she collected and nicknacks she'd brought back from some of her trips. There was also a small trunk at the end of the high poster bed in which, Aunt Wilma told her, she kept her "treasures." Whenever May asked her if she could look inside, her aunt would just say, "Some day, when the time is right, but not yet." It sounded like a delicious secret of some kind.

Wilma accompanied May back across the lawn to the Chandlers' porch, where Annie had brought a tray of lemonade and cookies. May went to play on the swing Walt had fixed for her on the low branch of the oak tree, while the two sisters talked in low voices.

When Annie had confided what had happened, Wilma said thoughtfully, "Well, I warned you it would be best to tell May she was adopted before some busybody did. Now, don't you think you should explain everything to her?"

"I just can't, Wilma. She's still too young. She'll forget about this. Children get over things. I don't want her to know she has parents somewhere who didn't want her, who gave her up. Wouldn't that hurt worse?"

"You can't protect her forever. She got hurt today in *kindergarten,* didn't she?"

"I understand what you're saying, but still—" Annie paused. "Walt doesn't want her to know either. You know he simply adores May."

"It may be worse in the long run if you don't."

Although May overheard some of what her mother and aunt were saying, she didn't understand them. That night her father brought home a quart of ice cream. Her mother made cupcakes, and May was allowed to lick the spoon.

For the rest of the week Annie kept May home from kindergarten until after Betty Sue's birthday party. Then May's life at school resumed apparently as before.

However, if May forgot about the incident, Annie and Walt did not. They started making plans to protect their adopted daughter from further hurt.

May was unaware of the many conversations between Wilma and Annie, or of Walt and Annie's discussions that followed the incident of the birthday party. The Chandlers were determined not to reveal to May that she was adopted. An unexpected opportunity helped strengthen that resolve. Walt was a pharmacist, and when he learned that a drugstore in Cedar Falls, a town about fifty miles north of Emeryville, was up for sale, he jumped at the chance to buy it. It was just the safeguard they were looking for—to bring May up in a town where no one knew she was adopted.

The move came as a surprise to May, but in September 1899, when May would have started first grade in Emeryville, she was enrolled in the Cedar Falls Elementary School instead.

May was sad to leave Aunt Wilma and Uncle Joe. Still, it was an exciting day when their furniture and boxes were loaded up to take to their new home in another town. Aunt Wilma cried and Uncle Joe's watery blue eyes glistened with tears when May hugged them good-bye. "We'll miss seeing you every day, darling,"

Aunt Wilma said, "but your mama promised to let you come for weekends sometimes."

In Cedar Falls the Chandlers moved into a pretty house in a pleasant tree-shaded neighborhood, next door to the Bancroft family. The day they moved in, Mrs. Bancroft brought over a freshly baked apple pie to welcome them.

Sheila Bancroft was very friendly and outgoing. She told Annie her husband worked at the local bank, and they had a daughter, Becky, age twelve, and a son, Loren, age eleven. Both were too old to be playmates for May, but they would be attending the same school.

That evening May heard Annie say, "I think we did the right thing, Walt. I'm sure we'll be very happy here. Mrs. Bancroft even mentioned she thought May resembled *me!*"

Although the Chandlers thought the move would be a clean slate and a new start for all of them, May had problems at Cedar Falls Elementary School. At seven, she had become very shy and found it difficult to make friends. Annie realized something was wrong. Had May unconsciously absorbed some of Annie's anxiety and overprotectiveness?

After nearly two months at her new school, May came home one day looking wistful. Annie asked her, "Wouldn't you like to bring someone home after school or ask someone to spend the day on Saturday?"

May replied sadly, "You have to have a best friend. I miss Miranda. We used to be best friends."

"Well, dear, there must be some nice little girl at this school you could get to know."

"Everyone pairs off at recess or picks each other for hopscotch teams." She sighed. "But first you have to have a best friend."

"Then why don't you get one?"

"Everyone's already taken," May explained patiently. "Besides, *you* have to get asked, and no one asked me."

Annie fretted and discussed it with Wilma many times on the phone. May overheard her and knew her lack of friends worried her mother, but there was really nothing she could do about it.

Loren Bancroft, the boy next door, was often outside his house working on his bicycle or folding newspapers to take on his delivery route. He was always friendly, and May took to talking to him. When February came, she confided her big fear.

"I know I'm not going to get any valentines," she said resignedly.

"How come?" Loren asked.

"'Cause I don't know anyone really well in my class. There's a big decorated box by the teacher's desk that people put them in, and then on Valentine's Day they're passed out. I know I'm going to be so embarrassed."

"You might be surprised. Get lots."

"No. I know I won't."

"Are you sending any?"

"Mama got me stuff to make them with—you know, colored paper and lace paper doilies—but I don't know . . ." Her voice trailed off uncertainly.

"Go ahead. Make 'em and send 'em," Loren advised.

"Well, maybe . . ."

At least she had fun making them. She took one for everyone in her class and when no one was paying attention, slipped them into the box in her classroom.

On Valentine's Day when she came in through the front gate, Loren shouted over the fence, "Hey, there, May, get any valentines?"

She held up a batch.

"See, I told you, didn't I?"

"Yes, but yesterday the teacher told the class that we should send valentines to everyone in the class." She stopped and leaned over the fence. "Some people got a bunch more than I did."

"But it wasn't like you thought, was it?"

"No." May had to agree. She was beginning to realize how smart Loren was. He knew so many things she still had to learn, and he was awfully nice.

When she went in the house, she found her mother was just taking a pan of heart-shaped sugar cookies out of the oven.

"You got a valentine, honey," Annie told her. "It was in the mailbox when I went to get the mail."

"I did?" May took the red envelope her mother handed her. Upon opening it she saw a picture of a basketful of puppies. The mother dog had a bandana tied over her eyes and was walking away holding one puppy dangling from her mouth. Inside it read, "Even in a blindfold test, I'd pick you from all the rest." It was signed, "Guess who."

Penfield, 1899

Life went on happily for April with the Barstows until October 1899. Peg and April were planting bulbs for spring. April loved to work alongside Peg, but lately something began to worry her. After only a short time, Peg would get pale and breathless. With obvious effort she would get up from her knees and walk shakily over to the back porch. She would sit down on the steps, lean against the post, take off her wide-brimmed sun hat, and fan herself. "Oh, my, April, I think I've had enough for one day. I'm too tired to do more. Don't know why that should be. We've hardly been out here twenty minutes."

The same thing happened more and more often. Many of the packets of seeds they'd had so much fun ordering from the seed catalogue in the winter remained un-planted. Often April found herself out in the garden alone. She worked harder than ever, doing double duty, weeding and watering. Sometimes Mama sat on the porch swing, giving her directions in her gentle voice. But little by little as the summer ended, Peg didn't come out at all. Now she took both a morning nap and one in the afternoon, sometimes not getting up until it was time for Daddy Ned to come home from work in the evening.

Then one terrible day Mama lay white and still on the bed in her room and told April she had to go to the hospital.

"Why, Mama, why?"

"So they can make me better. It won't be for long, sweetie. I promise. I'll be back."

But she couldn't even walk down the stairs and out to the buggy. Daddy Ned had to carry her. April stood watching, tears streaming down her face. She followed them out, and after Mama was seated inside the buggy, April climbed up to hug her. Peg cupped her cheek with one cold hand. "Don't look so sad, sweetie. Don't cry. Be a brave girl. I'll be home again soon."

April sat on the porch steps, waiting. Surely Daddy would be back soon. He had promised. April shivered. It was getting windy, cold. Soon it would be dark. She peered down the road. *When was he coming?* She played a little guessing game. *He'll be home after the next three vehicles pass,* she told herself. A farm wagon, a hay rack, and a horse-drawn carriage went by, then a buggy. But it wasn't Daddy Ned's. Not yet. She started over.

It was beginning to get dark when Mrs. Simmons came out on her porch and saw April. She called from over the fence, "You, there, April. You better come over here, stay inside, till your Pa gets home. It's pretty near supper time, and you can't sit out there in the dark. When he comes we can see him from my kitchen window."

Reluctantly, April stood up. She cast a longing glance down the empty road, then slowly walked toward the Simmons' house. Mrs. Simmons was probably right. It *was* getting cold. And it wouldn't be long. Surely Daddy Ned would come soon.

Mrs. Simmons cut her a piece of warm gingerbread and gave her a glass of buttermilk to drink. Then she showed April where she could sit at the window so she could see the road. There April sat and waited, and waited, and waited.

Mr. Simmons came home from work, and April overheard part of their whispered conversation.

"Barstow's bound to come back sometime."

"I don't know. All I know is we can't keep her—"

It grew dark outside, and April finally fell asleep on the Simmons' couch. When she woke up the next morning, Mrs. Simmons told her the terrible news. Mama was dead. Daddy Barstow had gone away. Where, they didn't know.

"They say he went plum crazy. His heart was broke—" Mrs. Simmons shook her head.

April felt her heart break too. Mama dead. Daddy gone. What was to become of her?

Two days later the county agent came and took April to the County Orphanage.

County Orphanage, 1900

The County Orphanage housed orphaned and abandoned children from the surrounding towns of Emeryville, Cooperstown, and Penfield until they were fifteen years of age. It was there April found herself, tearful, bewildered, and resentful.

She hated everything about the orphanage. She hated the coarse cotton dress she had to wear under the blue pinafore, the black wool stockings, and the high-top black shoes she had to lace up every morning. She hated marching everywhere in a line and eating at the long tables in the bleak dining room with all the noise and clatter.

She missed Peg and the little house she had made so bright and pretty with colorful curtains, pillows, and flowers. She missed it all so dreadfully it was like a cold, hard knot in her stomach and a bruise on her heart. At night in the dormitory, while lying on her narrow cot, April stuffed the corner of her lumpy pillow in her mouth to stifle the sobs that racked her small body. Where was Daddy Ned? Why didn't he come to get her? She longed to be cuddled in Mama's tender arms, to be kissed good night. Over the lump in her throat she tried to hum the melody to the lullabye Peg had sung to her every night before she went to sleep—"Lullabye, and good night, may the angels attend thee." *Where were the angels in this awful place?* April wondered.

The first week crawled by, then the second, then still another. Surely Daddy Ned would come soon. She stubbornly told the other children, "I'm waiting for my Daddy." Even when they hooted and hollered back, "Oh, sure!" she stuck to her story. And she believed it. Maybe he was on the road because of his job selling farm equipment, but he always came back. He would this time too. But slowly the weeks turned into a month, and still Daddy Ned didn't come. April began to lose hope, but she would never admit that, especially not to Jenny, the orphan girl with whom she shared laundry duty.

Gray light slanted in from the narrow windows of the basement laundry room where the two girls were working. A long table along one side held piles of folded sheets and two baskets still filled with sheets they had brought in from the clothesline.

At some remark of Jenny's, April replied, "I'm not going to be here that much longer." She pulled another sheet out of the basket. "My father is coming to get me soon," she said firmly as she secured the sheet under her chin and creased it in half.

"Sez you!" retorted Jenny. "You think you're different from the rest of us, but you ain't."

"I am, and I can prove it. He'll come, wait and see."

Jenny took one of the sheets out of the large basket and started to fold it. She gave April a scathing look. "You're kiddin' yourself if you think that. Your dad dumped you jest the same as what happened to most of us. Why else do you think you're here?" Not waiting for April to answer, Jenny stuck out her tongue and said, "I'll tell you why. 'Cause you're an orphan, that's why. Nobody wants orphans."

April pressed her lips together and willed herself not to cry. Even though Jenny's words stung and she had an awful feeling deep down inside that what Jenny said might be true, April wasn't going to give Jenny the satisfaction of having made her cry. Besides, Jenny was bigger and tougher, and one thing April had learned from being in the orphanage was that you don't pick a fight with someone bigger and stronger. She had also learned it wasn't smart to brag about something you weren't sure of. She had done a lot of bragging about how Daddy Ned would soon come for her, but now she was beginning to doubt it herself.

Then one day Mr. Dillon, the director of the orphanage, sent for April. His secretary, Miss Shelby, opened the office door for her. "There's someone here to see you."

To her shocked surprise, Daddy Ned was sitting in a chair opposite Mr. Dillon. The minute she saw him, April flung herself into his arms and cried, "Daddy Ned!" After a minute he pushed her gently away, put both hands on her shoulders, and looked at her. "My, April, you've grown. Must be two inches. You look different."

He looked different too. His eyes were red as if he needed sleep, and there were dark circles underneath them. His handsome face was puffy, and new lines surrounded his mouth. But it didn't matter. What mattered was that he was here. He had come to get her, just like she'd told the other orphans.

"Oh, Daddy! Can we go home now?"

Ned bit his lower lip. He shook his head and slowly said, "I'm afraid not, April. That's what I've come to tell you."

At this point Mr. Dillon got up from behind his desk and walked quickly to the door. "I'll leave you two to yourselves," he said and went out of the room.

April looked at Ned. He took one of April's hands in his own and rubbed her fingers. "Look, honey, I'm sorry I stayed away so long and didn't come to tell you—about Mama. I was too—" He stopped, cleared his throat. "Well, I went off my rocker for a while. You see, honey, now that Mama is gone, there's nobody—" his voice broke, "—nobody to take care of you anymore. I can't. Not with my job and all . . ."

April blinked. She felt her heart pinch. What did Daddy mean? Was he going away again? Was he not going to take her with him? Fear clutched her so hard she could hardly breathe. She had to do something to stop him. She swallowed hard. "Well, I can take care of myself. And I can cook. Mama taught me. I can fix our meals."

"But you're just a little girl, April." Ned's voice was husky. "It wouldn't work, not with me travelin' out in the boondocks, out of touch. If anything happened . . ." he broke off. "I tried to find a way—I even asked Ma if she could keep you while I was on the road but—" he halted.

April shuddered. Almost worse than the orphanage would be staying with Mrs. Beiderbaum. She had never been so afraid. "Please, Daddy, don't leave me here," she begged in a shaky voice.

"There's nothing else I can do, honey."

Ned put his head in both hands, rubbing his eyes with his fists. His broad shoulders shook a little.

April felt shivery and sick, like she might choke or throw up.

"Please, Daddy," she said again.

"Don't make it any harder for me, April." Ned got to his feet, stumbling a little. "It's no good. This is the best place for you, April."

With that he took a few quick strides to the door and yanked it open. He turned and looked back for a long moment, then jammed his felt hat on his head and went out the office door, letting it slam shut behind him.

April wanted to scream, but nothing came out of her throbbing throat. She was left with an ache that would never stop hurting, a pain that would never go away, a feeling of loss that would stay with her forever.

7

County Orphanage, 1905

April shoved the drawer of the file cabinet shut hard.

At the metallic sound of the slamming, Miss Shelby winced and put her hands over her ears. "My land, child, do you have to be quite that noisy?" She turned around from her desk to peer over her nose glasses at April.

At fourteen April was smart and quick. She outpaced her fellow orphan schoolmates and was bored by the regular curriculum. In exasperation the teachers recommended she be given some kind of job to keep her from causing mischief in the classroom. She was assigned to help Miss Shelby in the director's office. Even Miss Shelby was often hard put to keep April busy enough. Filing was one way—a job April hated.

"What ails you anyway, child? You've been goin' around with a face like a thunder cloud for the last couple of days."

"This work is so boring, Miss Shelby. How can you stand it?"

"Why do you think I told Mr. Dillon I needed office help?" the secretary replied with a hint of humor. "I thought someone else could file those manilla folders. I've been doin' it for years."

"How can you work at something you hate for years? I certainly don't intend to."

"Huh, I've heard ducks quack before, miss," Miss Shelby retorted and went back to the forms she was filling out.

"I want to do something exciting, interesting."

"And just what might that be?" Miss Shelby asked.

"If I could go to high school and get a diploma then there are any number of things I could do."

"Well, that's all to be seen. You have to pass the entrance exam first, you know. Right now I'm going over these requisitions for summer jobs. Now that you're fourteen, you're eligible to work on the outside, April. Here's a farm family that wants a mother's helper. The Schulzes. You're good with the younger children here. Want to give it a go?"

April hesitated. It would be great to get beyond the wire link fence and gray walls of the orphanage. And she loved being outdoors. Mama had given her a love of plants and gardening. A farm might be a place she would enjoy. Anything sounded better than this stuffy office.

April took the application Miss Shelby handed her.

From it April read out loud, "Job requirements: Help with household chores, laundry, cooking, oversee children, various other duties of rural life."

"The Schulze farm is pretty far out from town," Miss Shelby told her. "You'd have to live in."

"How many children?"

"Four and a baby."

Hmm, that might not be so bad. Maybe she'd have a room of her own. A nice change from sleeping in the dormitory with a dozen other girls. Fresh air, sunshine, animals, lots of vegetables and fruit to eat, rich milk and cream, real butter. The more she thought about it, the better it sounded.

But it did not turn out the way she imagined. Life at the Schulze farm was worse than at the orphanage. Far from being an idyllic rural setting, the Schulzes' farm was rundown, the house a shambles. The children were unkempt, misbehaved, their mother was ill-tempered, worn-out, and her husband was foulmouthed to his family and abusive to his animals.

Her duties were also heavier and harder than the Schulzes had described in their application for an employee. She had to be up at dawn, build the fire in the huge kitchen stove, then go out in the farmyard to feed the chickens, slop the hogs, and muck out the stables.

The Schulzes had not been truthful about the five children either. To April's dismay, besides the eight-month-old baby, two were still toddlers. They all had dirty faces, runny noses, and soggy diapers. She had full charge of the baby. To keep her from crying constantly, April had to carry her around on her hip while she did her other chores. The other children trailed behind her everywhere, nagging, whining, and fussing. Mrs. Schulze's usual way of communicating with her children was by screaming. Mr. Schulze was even worse. His loud voice was harsh and his words were punctuated with threats and swearing.

At night April climbed wearily up to the cramped loft that was her "private bedroom." There she dropped exhausted onto a straw pallet only to awaken at first light to begin the whole routine over again. Nobody was going to rescue her. Whatever happened from now on was up to her.

One day it all became unbearable. Everything that could go wrong did. When April went out to feed the barnyard animals, the gander in the flock of geese, who had always been mean, took off after her. Squawking loudly, flapping his wings ferociously, he chased her, nipping at her heels. April ran as fast as she could to get away from his sharp beak, but she tripped, almost dropping the pail of corn feed. Most of the contents spilled out. As she struggled to get the gate open and out of harm's way, the hook didn't catch, and the pigs came rushing out. This brought the vicious rooster off his perch to join the fray. Suddenly, Mr. Schulze was on the back porch yelling, "You stupid, no-count orphan! Ain't you got no sense?"

April flung down the half-empty pail, put her hands on her hips, and giving the man a furious glare, yelled back at him, "You're the one who's stupid and mean and no-count. You don't know how to take care of your children or treat your animals right."

Mr. Schulze turned red then almost purple. He shook his fist angrily at April. If he had had on his boots, he probably would have taken off after her. But in his bare feet he could only stamp his feet in rage, shout obscenities, and wave both arms.

April knew she had no choice. Either she stayed and continued to take this kind of treatment, or she left. She didn't know what Mr. Dillon, head of the orphanage, would say, or Miss Shelby for that matter, but she didn't care. Without a backward look at the angry farmer, April walked down to the gate and onto the road. She walked all the way back to the orphanage. She arrived with blistered feet and a resentful spirit but also with the determination that she would never allow anyone to treat her like that again.

Mr. Dillon, however, was angry. "You'll give our orphans a bad name by leaving a job," he fumed. Miss Shelby was more sympathetic. "You're smart, April. With or without a high school diploma, you could hold down an office job. When you leave here, I'll give you a recommendation."

"Thanks, Miss Shelby," April said, but inwardly she groaned. There must be something else she could do. This kind of humdrum, miserable work couldn't be her fate. Soon she would be old enough to leave the orphanage. Her head was full of plans and dreams. She couldn't wait to do something interesting.

1907

April passed the local high school entrance exam. She could live at the county home while going to school, but she had to work for her room and board there. That meant helping in the orphanage kitchen, scrubbing floors or doing other menial chores. This, combined with her studies, made for a long, hard day. April soon discovered that what she had taken on was proving more difficult than she had anticipated.

At age fifteen most of the girls at the county home left to go out on their own. April, however, had stood out in the orphanage school. But although she was naturally bright and quick to learn, she had not received the foundational schooling her classmates had. As a result, she had to work harder just to keep up.

Every day at school she also faced humiliation from her fellow students. Snubs and sneers, remarks and comments about orphans were common. April was too proud to let them know she overheard, but the remarks about her clothes, which came from the piles of donated clothes regularly sent to the orphanage, really hurt. April was clever with a needle and picked through the dismal bunch for things she could alter or remake. But there was nothing April could do about the handed-down shoes, which had worn soles and were often too big or too small. All in all, it took all the grit she could muster to face the daily assault on her self-esteem.

Some days as she trudged home from school back to the orphanage, April wondered if all her effort was worth it.

One particular day after school, April ran into Jenny, her old adversary from the laundry room.

"So how's little Miss Scholar?" Jenny taunted.

April started to ignore her, but Jenny caught her arm. "Listen, Miss Smarty, Know-It-All. I'm going to Bridge-port to get a job in the textile mill. They pay three dollars a week, and you can keep it all yourself." Jenny tossed her head and demanded, "Ain't that a lot better than havin' to toe the mark here and go to that silly school in town?" Jenny's jeering question echoed down the hall after her.

April bit back an angry rebuttal. She had to get to her job in the kitchen, then she had two hours to get all her homework done for the next day. All the time she was washing dishes, Jenny's words lingered in her mind.

The more she thought about it the better it sounded—and the more discontented April became. She was sick of feeling poor among her smug classmates. She began to envy Jenny sailing off to a life of freedom, no one telling her what to do, having her own money to spend.

If she went to Bridgeport, she could get a job just like Jenny. She'd be on her own with money in her pocket. No one could tell her where to go, what to do, or what time to do it. How hard could it be if Jenny could get such a job? Best of all, nobody would ever even have to know she was an orphan.

It didn't take April long to make up her mind.

When she told Miss Shelby, the secretary shook her head. "I'm sorry to hear this, April. But it's your decision. You've tried and worked hard, but I can't say I blame you."

Miss Shelby saw her off with plenty of advice about taking up with strangers and of regular church attendance.

"Now, you mind your p's and q's, April. You've got a good head on your shoulders, so be sure to use it."

"I will," April assured her. "Don't worry about me."

"Well, I *will* worry." Miss Shelby sniffed suspiciously, then blew her nose. "I worry about all you orphans, whether you think so or not." She patted April's shoulder and, tucking a dollar bill into her hand, said in a choked voice, "Good-bye and God bless."

With her small valise clutched tightly in one hand, April walked out the door of the County Orphanage without a backward look. She never wanted to see that ugly brick building again as long as she lived.

55

At the train station she bought her ticket then stood on the platform waiting for the train to Bridgeport. Suddenly a strange sensation swept over her. There was something familiar about this place, as if she'd been here before. The yellow frame station house. The smell of coal dust and the gritty feel of cinders. The wind blowing in her face and eyes. She felt a frightening sense of loss, of being separated. How odd. This was the first time she had taken a train trip—wasn't it?

April's heart began to pound. Her chest felt tight, and she couldn't seem to draw a deep breath. Her throat suddenly thickened with a lump. What was the matter with her? Thoughts of Mama and Daddy Ned came rushing into her mind. She hadn't allowed herself to think of her life with the Barstows for a long time, but now she felt sad and homesick. Her heart felt bruised with a hurt that she knew would never really go away.

But she had to be brave. What was the last thing Mama had said to her that day when she was taken to the hospital? "Be a brave little girl, April."

Well, she wasn't a little girl any more. And she would be brave. What was there to be afraid of anyway? Everything was going to be fine. She was going to get a job, make good pay, and be on her own—at last.

9

Cedar Falls, 1906

It was beginning to get dark as May bicycled home from the library one February afternoon. She had just turned into the Chandlers' driveway when a familiar voice called out to her.

Immediately her heart began to beat fast. Loren! She saw his tall, lanky figure emerge around the side of his house. He was twirling a ball in his hands, and she guessed he had been shooting baskets. Loren was on the high school's varsity team and had been named all-county champion this season.

May knew all about Loren. She kept a secret scrapbook of articles about him not only from the school newspaper but also from the sports page of the local daily.

"Hello, half-pint," he greeted her with the nickname he had given her that she'd come to resent. He considered her just "the little kid next door," exactly what she didn't want him to think about her.

"Don't call me that!" she retorted. "I don't like it."

"Then what do you want to be called? Pip-squeak?" He grinned.

Frustrated, she stuck out her tongue at him. She started wheeling her bike up the drive to park it, tossing her head as she tried to pass him. But Loren jumped into her path and reached out and took hold of one of the handle bars. "Whoa! Don't get mad. I was just teasing."

May tugged at the bike in an attempt to loosen his grip, but instead the bike tipped, causing some of her books to fall out of the basket. Loren bent to pick one up. He turned it over and looked at the title. "Hey, what have we here? Poetry? Is this a class assignment or for pleasure reading?"

May made a grab for the book, but Loren held it out of her reach. "Wait, let's see." He turned away and flipped open the book. "Here we go, Elizabeth Barrett Browning. How do I love thee, let me count the ways."

"Give that back to me, Loren Bancroft!" May demanded, running toward him and letting her bike fall over. But Loren was used to dodging players on the basketball court and was too fast for her.

Embarrassed and indignant, May felt tears sting her eyes. "You're nothing but a big bully!" she screamed.

Loren stopped short. He realized his teasing had gone too far. Quietly, he handed her the poetry book. "I'm sorry, May. I was just—" he halted. "I wasn't making fun of you. Honest. I think it's great that you like poetry."

She turned away. She picked up the rest of her library books and, leaving her bike where it had fallen, walked into her house without looking back.

The next week was Valentine's Day, and when May got home from school, she found a big, red envelope addressed to her. It was a large, fancy, store-bought card, but inside was a message scrawled in boyish handwriting. "Just in case you didn't get any other valentines, here's one just for you. This is to say I'm really sorry. Guess who."

May felt a smile tremble on her lips. No problem figuring out who the sender was. Now she also knew who had sent the valentine she had received long ago her first year in Cedar Falls, the one she had tucked away and cherished all these years, the one that read, "Even in a blindfold test, I'd pick you from all the rest."

1907

From her bedroom window, carefully concealed by the lace curtain, May watched Loren Bancroft leave the house next door. He looked extremely handsome, she thought, dressed in a suit for his senior prom. He was carrying a green florist box containing, May was sure, a lovely corsage for the girl he was escorting to the social event of the high school year. May sighed. Lucky Sarah Jane Palmer.

May would have given anything to trade places with her, even for just this one night. Ever since the Chandlers had moved to Cedar Falls and into the house next to the Bancrofts, May had idolized Loren. To him, of course, she was just the little girl next door whom he treated with the careless affection of a big brother.

In her deepest heart, May hoped some day he would see her in a different way. He wasn't that much older. Maybe in time the years that separated them wouldn't seem as great. Until then, she could dream, couldn't she?

She saw him dust off the leather seat of his father's automobile. Probably to make sure not a speck of dirt got on Sarah Jane's party dress. Then he hopped behind the wheel and with a loud cranking of the motor drove off down the street. Wistfully, May watched him turn the corner and disappear. She felt like Cinderella left at home while the others went off to the ball. If wishes on stars came true and prayers were answered, some day things might change between her and Loren. Until then, she could dream and keep a scrap of hope nestled deep in her heart.

1909

That summer Loren had a job as a counselor at a boys' camp in the Ozark mountains and was gone for two months. May missed seeing him, although he hardly acknowledged her existence. Rumor had it that Loren and Sarah Jane were going steady. May tried not to let it bother her, and she still clung to the dream that one day Loren would suddenly see her in a new way. May knew she was a dreamer and perhaps foolish to believe all the romantic novels she read and music she loved. But somehow she couldn't help it.

At least her summer was a busy one, so she didn't have lots of free time to think about Loren. She spent several weeks with Aunt Wilma in Emeryville, where she became part of the young people's crowd to which Miranda, her old kindergarten friend, had introduced her. She was invited to many of the picnics and parties they enjoyed and began receiving the attention of some of the young men in the group. At sixteen, May was a graceful girl with lovely eyes, a radiant smile, and lustrous maple-brown hair. She basked in this newfound admiration, but secretly she hoped Loren would take note when they both returned to Cedar Falls at the end of the summer.

May always enjoyed time spent with Aunt Wilma, who was more like a friend her own age than an adult— a loving, indulgent, kindred spirit. Wilma enjoyed May's company too, especially since Joe had died. May could do no wrong in Wilma's eyes. Wilma had bulging scrapbooks about May that were crammed with every crayoned picture, every laboriously printed letter or birthday card May had made, and snapshots of her at every age. All these she stored in her "mysterious" trunk, which she promised would one day belong to May.

10

1911

The bell over the door of Chandler's Pharmacy jangled. May looked over from where she stood at the cash register behind the cosmetic counter and saw Loren walk in. Her heart gave an excited little thump. She hadn't seen him much the past year except briefly when he had been home during the Christmas holiday. Her family had gone to Emeryville to be with Aunt Wilma, and by the time they returned, Loren had gone back to the university. Now he was home for spring break.

"Hello, May," he said as he sauntered toward her.

"Well, home is the hero!" she teased, pointing to the blue letter emblazoned on his white V-necked sweater that he had received for a college basketball championship. The news had been all over town.

Loren had the grace to look a little embarrassed, but he quickly recovered his casual manner. "It means a full athletic scholarship. That's the best thing about it." He paused. "What about you? Sis tells me you've won honors for English composition. I can't believe you'll be graduating this year."

May rolled her eyes dramatically. "Time flies when you're having fun, as they say, although I can't say high school has been all that much fun."

"Neither has college. You know I graduate this year too, then I'm supposed to be ready to face the workaday world. Looks as though you've already begun. How long have you been working here?"

"I started working Saturdays last year, and after I graduate it will be full-time, I guess. I like it. I enjoy seeing and helping people." She rearranged some cologne bottles in the display.

Just then the bell signaled the entrance of some other customers, and May saw two women enter the store. She glanced at them and then at Loren. Lowering her voice she asked, "Is there something I can help you with, Loren? If not, I'll have to go and wait on them."

"No, I mean yes. Well, I didn't come to buy anything. I—" He leaned closer over the counter. "I was wondering if you are planning to attend the church box supper tonight. And if you are, I wanted to know if you would like to go with me."

May's heart literally skipped a beat. She had been waiting for such a moment for a long time. Now when it was finally happening, she was at a loss for words.

"Why, Loren, thank you, but—" She paused. "You see, it is a box supper. That means the ladies in the guild fix boxes of food and they're auctioned off to the men. The money is for the missionary fund drive." Loren looked baffled. "What I'm saying is that if I went with you, I might not be able to eat with you. I have to eat with the person who bids on my box."

Loren laughed. "Oh, so that's how it works. Want to give me a hint so I can tell which box is yours?"

"That probably isn't fair, and the bidding might go higher than you want to pay."

"I'll take my chances. So how about it?"

"Miss, miss," a voice interrupted. "Would you please help me?"

"Right away, ma'am," May said, then whispered to Loren, "I have to go. I'll see you tonight."

May tried on and discarded three different outfits to wear that evening before deciding on a pink candy-striped dress trimmed with eyelet lace. Then she brushed and did her hair in three different styles before she was satisfied with the final effect.

"May, what on earth's keeping you, child?" she heard her mama's voice call up from the bottom of the stairs. "If you don't hurry, we'll be late and they will have already begun bidding on the box suppers."

"Coming, Mama!" May called back, and then after taking a last look at herself in the mirror above the bureau, she grabbed her handbag and knitted shawl and hurried downstairs.

65

When they arrived, the church hall was already crowded and noisy with people greeting each other and children running about chasing each other and laughing. Dozens of pretty ribboned and decorated boxes were lined up on long tables at the front of the room next to the podium where the auctioneer would take bids.

May glanced around, trying to see if she could spot Loren. What if he hadn't come? What if at the last minute he had decided to call on Sarah Jane Palmer instead? Then she saw him, and their eyes met almost as if he, too, had been searching the room for her.

May's heart flip-flopped, and she felt a catch in her throat. She had already begun to smile when Loren began crossing the room toward her.

A few hours later, Loren and May sat opposite each other at one of the tables in the festively decorated church hall.

"How did you know which box was mine?" May asked.

"I confess I cheated a little." Loren grinned, waving a drumstick as he spoke.

"Cheated?" May pretended to be shocked and wagged her finger at him playfully. "How did you manage that?"

"I ran next door after I left the pharmacy on the pretext of borrowing a cup of sugar for my mom, and I spotted your box all tied up with yellow and pink ribbons. Your mother had placed it on the hutch in the kitchen." He gave her a speculative look. "You surprised me. You're a good cook."

"I can't take much credit for this supper. Mama did the chicken, and the pecan cookies are Aunt Wilma's recipe."

"You're too modest. But what would you say your talents are?"

May thought for a minute. "I'm still trying to figure that out."

"Do you still like poetry?"

"Yes." She was quiet for a few seconds then said shyly, "That's what I won the award for—an original poem. It will be published in the yearbook." After she had told him, May blushed furiously. She didn't quite know why she had blurted that out. It seemed so prideful somehow. But the expression on Loren's face was so affectionate, his eyes so tender, that May felt he was exactly the person she wanted to tell. In fact, at that moment, she knew Loren was someone she could trust with the most precious things about herself, someone to whom she could tell anything.

During the next ten days, May's long-held dream became a reality. For the rest of Loren's spring break, they spent as much time together as possible. They took long walks and had long talks. They went on picnics and ate Sunday night suppers with their families. Loren would meet May after school each day and they would go to the soda parlor or to the town park. They never ran out of things to talk about. They laughed about the old memories they had of each other and discovered new, endearing qualities as well. It was a time of happiness and the awakening of love—confidences exchanged, promises made.

After Loren went back to school, letters flew back and forth between them. In June he was back in Cedar Falls to escort May to her senior ball and attend her graduation.

The Cedar Falls High School auditorium was filled with proud parents as the class of 1911 marched solemnly down the aisle and onto the stage to the music of "Pomp and Circumstance." No couple felt more pride and satisfaction than the Chandlers.

May had grown into a graceful young woman with lustrous light brown hair and a radiant smile. Annie knew some of the glow in May's face this evening was due to Loren Bancroft's arrival the night before. Obviously the two were in love. Annie couldn't be happier about May's choice and that everything was working out so well for her darling adopted daughter.

Even as the thought came, the word *adopted* brought a pang of guilt to Annie's heart. Had Wilma been right? Should she and Walt have told May the truth? Immediately, as the doubt arose, conviction that they had done the right thing followed. May was as much their daughter as if she'd been born to them, and she could have no memory of another life. After the first week or two, May had never uttered the name "Cissy" again nor burst into tears without any reason.

May had grown up secure in the love that she was wanted and cherished, never questioning her shadowy origin. Annie calmed herself. It was needless to stir up old questions. It had all worked out perfectly. May was facing an even happier future with a man who cared deeply for her and would continue to protect her.

Later that evening when Loren brought May home from her graduation dance, they sat on the front porch swing, rocking gently.

Loren put his arm around May's shoulder, drew her close, and kissed her on the cheek. Then he spoke the words May had long dreamed of hearing.

"You know I've fallen in love with you, don't you, May?"

"I love you too, Loren," she said. Then she laughed quietly and asked, "What took you so long to tell me?"

He kissed her again and said softly, "I guess I was just waiting for you to grow up."

Cedar Falls, 1913

If May Chandler seemed to have a charmed life, that changed drastically in the two years after her high school graduation. Both her parents died within six months of each other. Then when May was beginning to slowly recover from this shock, Aunt Wilma died.

Three weeks after the funeral, Loren took May to the train station. Wilma had left her house and all its belongings to May, who would now have to go through everything and ready the house to be sold. She and Loren planned to use the proceeds from the sale to purchase a home when they got married.

"I still think I should go with you, May. I don't like the idea of you going over there by yourself, staying in that empty house alone." Loren sounded anxious.

"I'll be fine, really." May reached up and with her finger touched his worried frown. Her engagement ring sparkled in the October sunshine.

"It's just that you've been through so much in the last few years—your mother's long illness, then your father's sudden death, now your aunt. It just seems too much for you to do all alone. Maybe I should go with you—"

"Please, Loren. I'll be fine. Aunt Wilma wouldn't have left it all to me unless she trusted me to make decisions about what to keep, what to dispose of—things you couldn't really decide for me. It's something I have to do alone. A labor of love really. I wouldn't want a stranger going through Aunt Wilma's personal things."

"You're right. I understand." Loren walked down the platform to where the conductor stood ready to help passengers onto the train.

Loren bent his head to kiss May. "I'll miss you terribly."

"I'll only be gone a week." She smiled.

He didn't remind her that due to all the family deaths, their wedding had already been postponed twice. He loved May dearly, and all these delays had made him impatient.

"All aboard!" the conductor shouted.

"I better go, Loren," May whispered and rose on tiptoe to kiss him again.

Settled in the coach, May pressed her face against the window and waved one small, black-gloved hand at Loren, who still stood on the platform.

It was only a short trip to Emeryville, a distance of about fifty miles. It was a trip May had taken often to visit Aunt Wilma and Uncle Joe. They had been like another set of parents to her all her life. She would miss them both almost as much as her mother and father. She was so blessed to have always been surrounded by so much love. And now she had her life with Loren to look forward to. After she completed her sad task at Aunt Wilma's, she and Loren could set a date for their wedding.

The train pulled into the Emeryville station, and May got off. She had walked a few blocks in the direction of her aunt and uncle's house when she heard someone call her name.

"May! May Chandler!"

She turned and saw a young woman wheeling a baby carriage and waving to her. May quickly recognized Miranda, her childhood friend. Miranda had married and moved away from Emeryville, and May had not seen her in nearly three years.

"Miranda, how good to see you!" May exclaimed. "And is this darling baby yours?"

"Yes, indeed. His name is Teddy. I'm here visiting my folks. What a coincidence to see you in Emeryville too."

"I'm afraid my visit is not the happiest of circumstances," May said.

"I know. I was sorry to hear about your aunt, May. She was such a sweet person. Will you be here long?"

"Just a few days to go through my aunt's belongings, get the house ready to sell."

"Would you have time to come over for tea and a visit? I know Mama would be happy to see you."

"I can't promise, Miranda. I don't know just how much there is to do. And I have to be back in Cedar Falls next weekend." She held out her left hand. "I'm engaged."

"That's wonderful! Who is he?"

The two friends chatted a bit longer, and May told her about her romance with Loren.

As the two friends parted ways, Miranda urged, "Do try to come and say hello to Mama. I often think of all the fun we used to have as children. And I'm so thrilled about your happiness—in spite of all you've been through lately."

"Thanks," May said gratefully and gave Miranda a hug.

May continued on her way, but walking along the tree-lined streets was a heart-tugging experience. At the corner was the yellow frame house with the white gingerbread trim where her aunt and uncle had lived. Next to it was the house the Chandlers had lived in until they had moved to Cedar Falls when May was six. The sight of both houses flooded her with warm, happy memories of her childhood.

Almost reluctantly, May mounted the porch steps, unlocked the front door, and went inside. The house felt too quiet and empty. It seemed strange not to hear Aunt Wilma's cheery "Hello," and no one welcomed her with a hug and a kiss. Maybe Loren was right, maybe she shouldn't have come alone.

She carried her suitcase upstairs and put it in the room Aunt Wilma always kept ready and waiting for May's visits. Aunt Wilma's bedroom door stood open, and May crossed the hall and looked in. Everything was just the same—the window shades and ruffled curtains just so, the big brass bed polished to a glistening shine with a handmade quilt neatly spread over it, and at the foot of the bed the small trunk, the one May always asked to see inside. May could almost hear Aunt Wilma saying, "Some day it will be yours to open and see for yourself."

Even though she had permission to open it, May approached the trunk warily. She knelt down on the floor in front of it and slowly lifted the lid.

On the shallow top shelf were a package wrapped in tissue paper and a large manilla envelope with Aunt Wilma's handwriting across the front. "To be opened only after my death," signed Wilma Rogers. May placed the envelope on the floor beside her and then opened the package. Turning back the layers of tissue she found a little pink smocked dress, a flannel coat and matching bonnet, and a pair of tiny white kid button shoes— clothes that would fit a two- or three-year-old little girl. Why had Aunt Wilma kept them? Had she had a baby who died? No one had ever said so.

Next, May picked up the manilla envelope. Maybe this would provide the answer. Curious, she undid the clasp and drew out a sheaf of yellowed newspaper

75

clippings. "Orphan Train Comes to Emeryville Bringing Homeless Tots to Place with Local Families." Clipped to the article was a picture of two little girls, dressed in matching outfits, similar to the set of clothes May had just discovered. May began to read the newspaper account. A trainload of orphaned and abandoned children had traveled from back East to be placed in Christian homes in the rural Midwest. May's hands began to tremble. She looked at the picture of the two little girls again. Out of the twenty children who had been on the train, why had Aunt Wilma kept this picture of these two? May studied the picture closely. There was definitely something familiar about the face of the smaller one. Why, of course, it looked like pictures of *her!* Her mother had had a professional photographer take a picture of her every year. They had been framed and placed on the mantelpiece at home. However, she couldn't recall seeing any pictures of her younger than age three. There were no baby pictures. Why? May took a long, shaky breath. Maybe because she had not been with the Chandlers her first three years? Is this what Aunt Wilma was trying to tell her? Had she been one of the orphans on the train? One of these two little girls in the picture? Had she been adopted or, as the article stated, "placed out" with the Chandlers? Did she have a sister? If she did, what had happened to her? And why had her parents never told her?

Well, there was someone who would have to know, someone who would have to be told. Loren. What would he think when he found out she was an orphan? What would his family think? To find out she wasn't the person they thought she was. That she was a nobody. Whatever happened, this was something that couldn't be hidden any longer.

With hands that trembled slightly, May began to put the contents of the envelope back where she had found them. It was all so terribly strange. As hard as she could she tried to remember the experience described by the newspaper reporter, but her mind was blank. When do childhood memories begin? She had been three at the time. Was that too young to remember the most important event in her life?

May looked at the picture once more, memorizing the other little girl's face so much like her own. Where was she? What kind of family had taken her? Did she know about May?

One thing May knew was that now she would have to find out. She would have to find her sister, wherever her search led, however long it took. But first she had to tell Loren.

12

At midnight May was still awake. Her mind was too restless, too full of questions for her to sleep. The shock of her discovery—that she was adopted and had a sister, that they had been on the Orphan Train—made sleep impossible. What should she do now? How should she go about finding her sister?

She bunched up her pillow, scrunched it under her head, and tried to think. Then the idea came. Tomorrow she would go to the *Emeryville Times* and ask to see the issue published on the day the Orphan Train arrived.

After a quick breakfast, May set out for the newspaper office. A clerk ushered her down to the "morgue," a basement room where old editions of the newspaper were stored according to year. There she found a large book containing copies of the newspaper for the year 1895. May opened it, scanning page after page. Tiny dust motes flew up from the yellowing paper, tickling her nose and making her sneeze.

At last she came to the front page of the issue in which the arrival of the Orphan Train was the headline story. At the end of the article was a list of the families with whom the orphans had been "placed out." With her heart racing, May traced down the list. She quickly found the name of her parents: CHANDLER, WALT AND ANNIE, girl, May, 3 years. Then she saw BARSTOW, NED AND PEG, girl, April, 4 years.

April! A little girl named April. That must be her sister. Sisters, fancifully named April and May! She whispered the names together, over and over. I'm May, and my sister is April. There could be no mistake. The little girls in the pictures were three and four. Only a year apart. Almost twins. Dressed in identical pink outfits by their real mother.

Tears crowded into May's eyes. *She must have loved us very much. Why, then, did she give us up to strangers?*

May returned the portfolio to the clerk at the desk and left. In her hand she clutched the scrap of paper on which she had jotted Ned Barstow, 62 Wesley Road. If the Barstows still lived there, it might be possible she would also find her sister there.

A row of rural mailboxes stood at the end of a narrow lane. Carefully, May guided the horse and buggy she had rented at the livery up the lane. Two houses were at the end. One looked deserted. In front of the other one a woman was working in her garden. She looked up curiously as May drove up.

"Good afternoon," May said politely. "Do you happen to know the Barstows?"

"The Barstows? They've been long gone, miss. Years! Nice folks." The woman shook her head. "It was really sad."

"Sad?" May wound the reins around the brake stick and got down from the buggy. "What was sad about it?"

"Well, they had a little girl about six or seven. He was a traveling man, sold farm equipment. His wife was a sweet thing, but frail. She got took bad and went to the hospital. Died there." The woman brushed back a straggling strand of hair from her perspiring forehead. "Barstow went plum crazy afterward, we heard. He disappeared after the funeral. The little girl stayed a day or two with us, but we thought it best to take her to the County Orphanage, figuring when he came to his senses he'd go there for her. But first thing we knew, he'd packed up most of their belongings and left. That's all I can tell you."

Disappointed but not discouraged, May followed the woman's directions and headed straight to the County Orphanage.

At first sight of the forbidding entrance, May imagined how little April must have felt arriving here. She had just lost her mother—her second one—so she must have been reeling from another terrible loss. And her father gone too. What a bewildered, frightened little child she must have been. May's heart ached for her sister.

Inside, May was met by a gray-haired woman who regarded her curiously. "I'm Harriet Shelby, the director's secretary. May I help you?"

At May's question, she peered over metal-rimmed nose glasses at her. "April Barstow? Why, she's been gone must be over five years. We don't keep them here past fifteen. We have no way of keeping track of them when they leave."

"Is there anyone who might know?"

"Why do you want to find her?"

"I believe we're sisters, and I'm trying to locate her."

Harriet Shelby's expression changed to one of sympathy.

"She set out for Bridgeport to get a job in the textile factory. Some of our girls do. I'm not sure that's what she did." A slight smile touched Miss Shelby's prim mouth. "April had ideas of her own."

"That's all you can tell me?"

"She had spunk. She walked away from one job we'd sent her to. A farm family called the Schulzes. Said she wouldn't stay. Stubborn she was. April had a mind of her own."

May started to leave then turned back. "Could you describe what she looks like? I only have a picture of her when she was four."

Harriet Shelby studied May intently for a minute.

"Well, I'd say sort of like you. About your height and coloring, but a lot thinner. Hard to say what she looks like now she's a grown woman." Miss Shelby hesitated then suggested, "You might find out more if you check the Orphan Train Society's headquarters in Boston. They send one of their agents every year to check on the children they place. They might have more information that could help you."

May left with more hope. It was a scary thought, but if she had to travel to Boston to find April, she would. On her way out, May passed by the orphans' playground and saw dozens of little children in their drab uniforms. *There but for the grace of God,* she thought to herself. She and April were orphans just like these. For some reason they had been abandoned, unwanted, placed out to whomever would take them.

She had been the lucky one—adopted by the Chandlers, raised in a loving home.

But what about April? Where was she? Until she found her, May knew she could never be completely happy.

Cedar Falls

Loren was waiting for May when she got off the train at Cedar Falls.

"I've missed you terribly, May." He kissed her then took the valise she handed him. "Is this all? I thought you planned to bring back some of your aunt's things you wanted to keep."

"I haven't finished. I have to go back." May met his disappointed look. "I came home only for the weekend. I found something I didn't expect, and well, there's something we have to talk about, something I have to tell you."

"What else is there to do? If it involves selling the house, maybe I'd better go with you this time. I've had some experience along those lines at the bank."

May shook her head. "It's nothing like that. It's something entirely different. Before we go to your parents' house, can we go somewhere to talk privately?"

Loren looked puzzled. "Mother's expecting us for supper," he began, but May's expression stopped whatever he was going to say. "If it's that important, of course. We could go to the park." His eyes showed concern. May slipped her hand through his arm.

"Yes, that's a good idea."

The park was a special place to them. It was where they had shared their first kiss, where they had become engaged. The tree-shaded setting, with its duck pond, arched stone bridge, and white lattice gazebo, provided a romantic spot for intimate conversations. It seemed to May the right place to discuss her discovery, one that would affect Loren almost as much as it affected her. How would he take the news that she had been one of the children on the Orphan Train?

When they were seated on a bench overlooking the pond, Loren asked, "What did you want to talk about?"

Now that the time had come, May couldn't get the words out. Tears spilled down her cheeks. "I don't know how to tell you."

Startled, Loren asked, "What is it, May? Are you breaking our engagement?"

May shook her head. "No, no, it's nothing like that. Nothing about you. It's about *me!*"

"What about you?"

In a few breathless sentences, May poured out her story. "I'm not who you think I am, Loren. I'm not a

Chandler. I'm an orphan. I came on the Orphan Train to Emeryville when I was just a young girl. I found it all in Aunt Wilma's trunk—newspaper clippings, pictures . . . Aunt Wilma had kept everything. She meant for me to know, meant for me to find out—"

The next thing May knew, Loren's arms were around her, holding her while she leaned against his shoulder, crying.

"I was afraid to tell you, Loren, afraid that once you knew, you wouldn't want me. You'd be ashamed. You'd think I was a nobody, from nowhere."

"May, how could you think that? Don't you know how much I love you? And besides, May, I already knew."

May drew back and stared at him. "You *knew?* About *me?* About me being an *orphan?*"

"Yes. Your father told me when I asked him to marry you. He wanted to know if it made a difference to me. But of course it didn't. It doesn't change anything."

"But it *does,* Loren. Don't you see that? It changes everything."

"Why should it, May?" Loren got a clean, folded handkerchief out of his jacket pocket and handed it to her to wipe her eyes. "I love you—what I know about you, *what* you are, *who* you are. That's all I need to know."

"I don't know why Mama and Papa never told me."

"Probably because they considered you their own. I don't know. People do what they think is best. Anyway, it never made any difference in the way they felt about you. So why should it matter now, May?"

"Don't you see? Can't you understand? Suddenly, to find out you're not who you think you are. And there's more, Loren. Among Aunt Wilma's things I found a newspaper clipping about the day the Orphan Train came to Emeryville, describing the children who were on it, the families who took them. There was a picture of two little girls. Sisters."

Loren regarded her steadily. "Yes."

"One of those children was me, Loren. The other one was—my sister. I have a sister I never knew about, never knew I had." She waited for his reaction. When it didn't come immediately, she went on. "She was adopted by another family, grew up somewhere else. I don't know where she is or if she even knows about me. That's why we needed to talk about it, Loren. I have to find her."

"How can you be sure the picture is of you and not some other little girls?"

"Because why would Aunt Wilma have kept the clipping, put it away with the other things for me to find? And the little girls' names were May and April. There was a story in the paper along with the picture that said our real mother had requested we be placed out together. Evidently, that wasn't possible and we were separated." May's voice broke, and she paused before going on. "That makes me so sad, Loren, to think she wanted us to be together and then we were separated and didn't even know each other existed. Or at least I didn't. That's why I've got to look for her. She was four years old at the time. She may remember something. Anyway, I've got to find her."

"But how?"

"Well, I do know the name of the people who adopted her. Barstow. First of all, I'll have to get the records from the Orphan Train people and find out their whereabouts. The newspaper article said they have to keep track of the children they place out for at least two years."

"Barstow." Loren frowned. "I don't know anyone around here with that name. May, this may be like looking for a needle in a haystack. After all these years. You say she was four then. Well, she'd be about twenty-two now. Maybe she's married and her name has changed. Maybe the Barstows changed her first name when they took her. April's not a very common name."

May's eyes misted suddenly. "I know, Loren. That's what makes me even sadder. I'm sure our real mother gave us these special names because she loved us. I don't know why she had to give us up, but she did want us to be together. I have to try to bring that about . . . even this much later."

"Your search might take a long time, and it may lead nowhere."

"That's the chance I'll have to take." May's mouth tightened firmly. "I have to find her. She's my sister." She hesitated. "That's why I had to talk to you, to tell you what I've decided to do." May placed her hand on his arm. "Don't you see, Loren? However long it takes, whatever I have to do, I must try."

"But if your parents had wanted you to know all this, wouldn't they have told you, not left it to happenstance for you to find out?"

"For whatever reason, they didn't. Evidently Aunt Wilma didn't agree with that decision. That's why she left me the information, so I could decide for myself." May pressed Loren's tightly clenched hands. "Oh, Loren, it's like finding a book in which the first chapters have been torn out, like a mystery waiting to be unraveled. All my life up to now has been based on something that isn't true. Not that anyone meant to lie or hurt me. Mama and Papa were wonderful parents, gave me a secure, happy childhood. But now I can't go on like I don't know."

"What if you're better off not knowing the truth about your sister?"

"That's a risk, I suppose. But the Bible says the truth sets us free. At least I'll have the satisfaction of having tried."

"What if your aunt made a mistake? What if those two little girls are two entirely different children?"

"I didn't tell you what makes me so sure." May drew a deep breath. "Auntie saved the clothes I wore when I came on the Orphan Train. A sweet, little, pink smocked dress and a matching ruffled bonnet. They were carefully wrapped in tissue paper in her trunk along with the packet of information. In the picture published in the newspaper the little girls were dressed in identical outfits—smocked dresses, ruffled bonnets."

Loren scowled. "Don't all little girls dress like that?"

"Their names were printed under the photo. May and April. Imagine, Loren. Two little girls named April and May." She leaned back and stared at him. "Don't you understand that I have to search for my sister?"

"But what about us? Our wedding? We've already postponed it twice. This might mean—"

"I know, but can't you see, my life isn't complete? I can't start a new life with you until I know my past. I must find my sister, no matter how long it takes."

The more they discussed it, the gloomier Loren became. But he could see May's mind was made up. There was no changing it. She would go to Boston alone. He couldn't take the time off work, and besides, the fact that they were not married would make traveling arrangements and accommodations awkward and expensive. May would have to go by herself.

A week later May and Loren were at the train station again.

"It seems we're always saying good-bye lately," Loren said gloomily. "Boston's such a long way for you to go. I wish I could help more."

"You are helping by letting me go."

"I just hope it's not a wild goose chase."

May winced. Loren was saying what she had not wanted to consider. "I have to try anyway. There must be records. We had to have real parents, Loren. There has to be some trace of them."

Loren drew her into his arms and held her tight. May sighed, leaning against the roughness of his tweed coat, wishing she could stay there safe and protected.

"Promise you'll be careful. Boston is a big city," Loren whispered as she lifted her face for his kiss.

In spite of his strong arms holding her, inside May felt more alone than ever. She was setting out on what might prove to be an impossible journey, leading only to a dead end.

Bridgeport

The sound of her alarm clock jarred April awake. She stirred on the lumpy mattress and slowly opened heavy-lidded eyes. She had stayed up late the night before working on one of her handicraft projects, and she had not slept well either. She stayed in bed for a minute wishing she could put the pillow over her head and go back to sleep. But that was impossible. She was due at the mill for the early shift at 5:00 A.M. She groaned, tossed aside the thin blanket, and sat up. She swung her legs over the edge of the narrow iron bed and shivered as her bare feet touched the cold floor.

She glanced over at the small table piled high with an assortment of materials: rolls of ribbon, yards of lace, cording, scraps of velvet and silk, all gleaned from the remnant sections of the fabric store. They were the resources April needed for the little business she was trying to build.

She had put to good use the skills Peg Barstow had taught her when she was a child. She was able to make a little extra money fashioning dainty corsages, headbands and hair combs, and ornaments for handbags. Lately, she had also been busy trimming hats for her fellow factory workers. Unfortunately, working twelve hours in front of a loom with two short breaks didn't leave her with much energy, especially since she'd caught a bad cold.

April dressed quickly. She'd have to leave her boardinghouse room right away if she wanted to stop for coffee at the small stand next to the mill gate before it was time to punch the time clock. The boss docked the girls for every minute they were late, and she couldn't afford that. It was difficult putting extra money aside, even though she didn't throw her hard-earned money away on cheap, flashy clothes or at the nickelodeon or dance hall as most of her fellow workers did. But no matter how she scrimped and saved, she couldn't seem to get ahead, to set aside enough money so she could quit her job at the mill. Room and board and a few other necessary expenses seemed to take all of her weekly paycheck. And there always seemed to be some unexpected expense, like the costly cough medicine she had been taking in big spoonfuls for weeks.

April took one last look at the hat she was trimming for one of her friends. She would much rather stay and complete the project than head for the mill. Thoughts of how she and Peg had worked happily together flashed through her mind, and she felt a sharp pang of regret. That brief time in her life had been so happy, and she missed the sense of joy with which she had met each day. Compared to the drabness of her present situation, the past seemed like a dream, a life lived by someone else.

April walked out of her room, shutting the door behind her, then she trudged down the narrow stairway, out the front door, and down the dark street toward the mill.

Plumes of murky smoke billowing out from the factory chimneys darkened the already gray, overcast sky. April pulled the collar of her threadbare coat closer around her neck, her head bent against the chilling wind. As she neared the mill, she looked up at the dirty red brick building with its blackened windows and shuddered.

She dreaded the thought of the next twelve hours ahead. She hated standing on the plank platform in the high-ceilinged, drafty room with the constant clacking of the wooden shuttles, the thump of foot pedals as the looms wove yard after yard of cloth. The stifling air filled with flying bits of thread and the smell of pungent dye burned the throat with every breath.

April had never planned to work at the Bridgeport textile mill for this long. Making money had sounded good to her at first, had planted optimism in her heart that she would be able to save enough money to eventually make her dream come true. Since her days in the orphanage, April had nourished a dream of having a milliner's shop of her own someday. She knew just how she would decorate it and how she would display her handmade merchandise. The store would have pretty hats in the window, and it would carry accessories such as scarves, gloves, fans, and hair ornaments to tempt shoppers.

But working long hours at the mill left little time to pursue her dream, and how would she ever save enough money to start her own shop? Lack of energy was also a big problem right now. Her cold had drained her of her usual pep. Just getting through a shift took a great deal of effort. Her dream now seemed farther away than ever.

April stopped and dug out a dime for a mug of coffee. She wrapped her cold hands around it to warm them and sipped the hot liquid. Soon the warning whistle announcing the beginning of the early shift split the air. April gulped the rest of her coffee, then hurried past the factory gates into the shelter that housed the workers' time cards. She quickly punched in and went inside.

Boston

May stood on the curb outside the Boston train terminal. At her request a red-capped porter hailed a cab to take her to the hotel where Loren's father had made reservations for her. She shivered in the cutting wind. She had been told Boston winters were fierce, and even this early in November it was freezing cold.

"Looks like we might have snow before morning," the cab driver said as May got out at the hotel entrance.

His prediction proved true. The next morning May woke up to a snow-blanketed city. But bad weather did not keep her from beginning her search. In a city directory she looked for a listing for the Orphan Train Society. She didn't find one, so she looked up the address of the Children's Welfare Department and then set out on her search.

Inside the large brick building a clerk directed her to the second floor, where she pushed through double doors into a large room crowded with people. She stood on the threshold for a minute, glancing around. Sitting on folding chairs and benches along the wall were mostly women with young children. Babies were crying, youngsters on the floor were tugging at their mother's skirts. The women looked worn, shabby, distraught—their gaunt faces and desperate eyes seemed to be seeking some kind of rescue. Had her mother been one of these? May's heart pinched.

May gave her name to an indifferent clerk sitting at a desk marked INFORMATION. "My name is May Chandler. I was put on an Orphan Train in 1895, placed out in Emeryville, Arkansas. My sister was with me but was adopted by another family. I'm trying to find her."

"Just take a seat. Miss Roth is the one you should see." The clerk pointed to the back of the room to a desk with an identifying sign WINONA ROTH.

It seemed ages before May's name was called. As she hurried forward, a weary-eyed woman looked up from behind a clutter of bulging folders. "Yes? What can I do for you?"

"Help me find my sister," May replied as she sat down on the edge of the chair beside the desk. She told her story quickly. At the names April and May she saw a flicker of change in the woman's expression.

"It all happened so long ago, but I do remember two little girls with those names. April and May. Not your everyday sort of name, right?"

Miss Roth stood up and went to her file cabinet. She opened a drawer and rifled through a number of folders before bringing one back to her desk. She put her fingers to her temples as though she had a headache, then she spoke in a firm tone. "Miss Chandler, I wish I could help you, but we have rules. Once a child is adopted we're not permitted to give out any follow-up information."

A long silence followed as if Miss Roth were trying to come to a decision. May leaned forward on the edge of the chair.

"Even when the children are adults?"

Miss Roth shook her head. Then she rose from behind the desk. "Excuse me for a minute. I have to speak to my supervisor."

She moved past May's chair and went into an inner office and closed the door.

The minute stretched into ten. May stirred restlessly. Where had the woman gone? To get some records? Check on some files? Get permission to give her more information? May got up and went to the window. Snow was still falling. Impatiently, May turned back. As she did so, her gaze fell on the desk. Suddenly May realized Miss Roth had left the folder open.

May cast a furtive look over her shoulder, then moved over quickly and read what was written on the first page.

April: birthdate, September 10, 1891
May: birthdate, July 22, 1892
Mother: Alisa Clarke   Occupation: Student
Father: Sebastian Revoc   Occupation: Musician
AUTHORIZED RELEASE FOR ADOPTION

There was only one signature: Alisa Clarke. A further bit of information was dated 1895. Both children placed on the Orphan Train, destination Emeryville, Arkansas.

Emeryville, Arkansas! May drew in her breath sharply. This was the confirmation she needed.

May's heart pumped wildly. Now she had her parents' names and written proof that she and her sister were sent to Emeryville and adopted there—May by the Chandlers, April by the Barstows. All at once she felt dizzy, almost as if she might faint. The door to the inner office opened, and Miss Roth returned. May sat back down. With her hands clenched in her lap, she repeated the names of her parents over and over in her head. Lest she forget? No, not ever. At last, she knew who she was.

"I'm sorry I could not give you more help, Miss Chandler. But I wish you the best," Miss Roth said, closing the folder and their interview. May walked stiffly to the front door, dazed by what she had learned. Once outside the building the cold air cleared the fuzziness from her brain. She tingled with excitement. She had the names of her real parents! Alisa Clarke and Sebastian Revoc. A musician and a student. Now she had proof that she and her sister were their children and had been put on the Orphan Train to Emeryville.

What her next step should be May wasn't sure. Go to Bridgeport, where Harriet Shelby told her April had headed? It was snowing heavily now. The flakes needled her cheeks with tiny icy pellets, so she decided to catch a trolley.

Back at the hotel May decided to look up her parents in the phone directory, see if either were listed. She first turned to the Cs, looking for an Alisa Clarke. But a student without enough money to support her two children could hardly afford telephone service. Besides, after twenty-five years, her name might be different. She might no longer live in the area. Next, May turned to the Rs. There a name leaped out from the page: Revoc, Sebastian. An address followed.

Jolted by the reality of his existence, May felt her knees wobble. Her father lived in Boston. Her mind raced. Revoc was a professional musician. Boston had its own symphony orchestra. Was he a member? It was also the location of a well-known music conservatory. Perhaps he was a teacher there? Had Alisa Clarke been his student? Is that how they had met? A romantic possibility, a tragic ending.

Now what? Should she contact Revoc? Identify herself? She bought a paper at the newstand and went up to her room. She took off her coat and hat, preoccupied by troubling thoughts. Should she try to contact her father? Her answer came sooner than she could have expected. In the second section of the newspaper in the events listing was a boxed announcement: "Benefit Concert for the Music Conservatory, Featuring Sebastian Revoc, Solo Violinist."

May's hands trembled. This had to be more than a coincidence. Was this a sign? The impulse to call her father was strong, but maybe that would be too much of a shock. Maybe writing him would be best. She went over to the desk, pulled out a sheet of hotel stationery, and dipped the pen into the inkwell. With the pen poised above the paper, May mentally worded the note then began to write.

> Mr. Sebastian Revoc,
> If you would like some information about your daughters, the children of Alisa Clarke, please contact me at the above address. I will be here until—

May halted. She could delay her departure only a few days or Loren would be upset. She wrote, "Thursday next." Then she signed the note "M. Chandler."

She slipped it into a matching envelope, addressed and sealed it. The next morning she left it at the front desk to be mailed.

Days went by with no reply. Why hadn't she heard anything? Had Revoc been too shocked? Too ashamed? Afraid of blackmail? Or maybe he was simply out of town on a concert tour.

As the days passed, however, May grew desperate. Her return train ticket to Cedar Falls had been purchased, and she had already changed her reservation twice. She had promised Loren she would be home for Christmas. She could not disappoint him. He had already been so patient with the many postponements of their wedding. Her trip to Bridgeport would have to wait.

Finally, the day she was scheduled to leave Boston, May went to the public phone in the lobby and gave Revoc's number to the operator.

A man's voice answered, "Mr. Revoc's residence."

May's voice was shaky. "May I speak to Mr. Revoc, please."

"This is his secretary. May I ask who's calling?"

May's hand clutched the ear instrument. Should she leave her name? Or say "his daughter"? She hesitated. He had had time to receive the letter, consider it, respond. Reality hit. Her father had evidently decided not to contact her. There was nothing more to do.

The secretary spoke again. "Would you care to leave a message?"

"No, thank you," May managed to say. "No message."

She hung up. It was as if she heard the slamming of a door that would never be opened—no matter how long or hard she knocked. Revoc was the key, still he would not unlock the door to the past. The fact was that she and her sister, if she ever found her, would always be orphans.

Cedar Falls, 1913

Christmas with the Bancrofts passed in a blur. May tried her best to enter into the festivities, to appreciate the beautifully trimmed tree, the carols and candles, even the beautiful midnight church service followed by the fruitcake and eggnog and lovely presents. But she was too distracted, too anxious to continue her search for her lost sister.

Finally, by New Year's Eve she told Loren she must go back East and continue to look for April.

"But what about *us*, May?"

"I'm sorry, Loren, but I can't give up now that I'm so close."

"Close? I don't think you're close. You still have a bunch of loose ends you may never be able to tie up."

"I have to find my sister."

Loren flung up his hands in a helpless gesture.

"Maybe she doesn't want to be found. Have you ever thought of that? She was the older one. She must remember you. Children of four have a memory. Why hasn't she looked for you all these years?"

"I can't explain any more, Loren. I just know I can't give up now."

Exasperated, Loren said, "Can't we at least set the wedding for June?"

May looked at Loren. She had been in love with him for so long. She couldn't risk losing him.

"All right, I agree."

Loren's expression softened. "Look, May, even if you haven't found your sister by then, after we're married, I'll help you. I will, I promise."

May knew Loren meant what he said. The question was did *she?* Could she really go happily on with their wedding plans if she hadn't found April?

Bridgeport, 1913

As soon as April started out, a fierce wind blew tiny darts of sleety snow against her face. She tightened the scarf wound around her neck, pulling it up to protect her cheeks. Her head bent against the wind, April thought to herself, *Maybe I should have stayed home on a day like this.*

But April loved Christmas. When she lived with the Barstows, it was one of the few times during the year when all three of them went to church together. April had never missed a Christmas service since leaving the orphanage and being on her own. Somehow it brought back all the good memories of that happy time in her life. She didn't dwell on the past much, not if she could help it. It made her too sad. But this was Christmas, and Christmas was special, no matter what.

The church was full, families mostly, April noted as she glanced around. Most pews contained a mother and a father with a group of little children wedged between them. April slipped into a side pew feeling very conscious of being alone.

The church smelled of cedar, candle wax, and a spicy mixture of bayberries and spruce that came from the garlands decorating the stained glass windows. The church was warm after her cold walk, and April's eyes began to water, or at least she told herself her eyes were just watering. She took out a hanky and wiped her eyes, then tried to concentrate on the stable scene to the right of the altar.

She remembered the first time the Barstows had taken her to church on Christmas and Peg had pointed out the baby Jesus in the straw-filled manger. April had been puzzled and asked, "Why does everyone have on warm clothes except him?" Peg explained that in real life his mother had wrapped him up and held him close to her own body to keep him warm. Peg was always able to answer April's questions.

April swallowed over the hard lump that tightened in her throat. She picked up a hymn book from the rack in front of her and tried to join in the singing of "Joy to the World," not that there was much joy in the world

April knew. But she held out hope that things would get better. One of these days . . . if she kept trying and working hard . . .

The thin layer of snow that had fallen during the service would soon turn gray from the sooty smoke that came from the factory furnaces and stacks. April shuddered. The service had been beautiful, and April was glad she had ventured out to attend. Peg would be happy that April was faithful to the seed she had planted, and that made April feel good. Whatever lay ahead, April always had those years to cherish.

It was late afternoon by the time May reached Bridgeport. The trip had been a "milk run," the train stopping at every small town along the way with long delays. She felt headachy and tired and, she had to admit, a little scared. Was looking for her sister like looking for a needle in a haystack, as Loren had said? May prayed not.

All she really had to go on here was the textile mill, Bridgeport's main industry that employed dozens of young women to work in the carting and weaving rooms. She would start there. But was April even still working there? She may have gone on to another job, another town. She may even be married, have another name.

But May felt she was on a mission. With no taxi in sight, she began walking down the narrow, gritty street leading away from the train station, praying for protection. Lately May had relied more and more on the Bible verses she had memorized in Sunday school.

A particular one had frequently come to mind. Joshua 1:9: "Be strong and of good courage; be not afraid, neither be thou dismayed: thy God is with thee whithersoever thou goest."

May squared her shoulders and walked briskly until at last she saw a drab-looking hotel. *Thank you, Lord!* she whispered and hurried toward it.

After an uncomfortable night on a lumpy mattress, May awakened. It was still dark outside, but she got up, dressed, and went down to the dining room. Her stomach was in knots, but she sipped some weak coffee and nibbled on a limp piece of toast. She learned from the desk clerk that the first shift at the factory ended at five o'clock. "You'll hear the whistle. It about splits your ear drums," he told her grimly.

She decided she would wait at the gate as the workers left for the day. Far-fetched as it seemed, May felt if April were among them she would recognize her. May had studied the picture of the two little orphans many times. They probably had retained the strong resemblance they had had as children. Miss Shelby at the orphanage had remarked that they were about the same height, build, and had the same coloring. It was *possible!*

The day seemed endless as May waited for the whistle signaling the end of the day shift. Shortly before 5:00, May grabbed the jacket of her suit, put on her hat, and hurried down the street. She began to walk faster, then broke into a half run.

She positioned herself at the gate where the departing workers exited the factory. Her heart pumped wildly as she searched for a face in the crowd that might be April's, someone who looked like herself. The stream of young women was passing so quickly that May panicked, afraid she might miss the one she hoped to find.

Then she noticed a tall young woman walking out the gate arm in arm with another worker. May's throat tightened. *There she was!* It was like looking in a mirror. The woman had wide hazel eyes and maple-brown hair pulled back from a lightly freckled face. Yes, May was sure. She quickly took a step into their path, halting them.

"Wait, please!" May said in a choked voice. "Could I speak to you for a minute?"

Both young women stopped and stared at May suspiciously.

"You mean *me?*" asked the one, touching her thumb to her chest.

"Yes."

"What for?"

"Please, I'd really like to talk to you. Could we go somewhere to talk—privately?"

"What about?"

"Well, I think maybe—I think we may be related."

The woman's eyes narrowed and traveled over May's fashionable outfit—the green knit suit collared and cuffed in beaver fur, the hat with its tilted brim. A doubtful smile touched her lips. "I don't think so—"

Her companion nudged her and gave a harsh laugh. "Hah! Some chance. We both come out of an orphanage."

"So did I!" May exclaimed. "That's what I want to talk to you about. Is your name April?"

The young woman looked startled, but her friend tugged at her arm. "Come on, let's go."

"Please, I've come a long way." May reached out her hand. " I really think we ought to talk."

She saw curiosity sharpen in the eyes so like hers. Hope sprang up in May's heart.

After a moment of hesitation, the one May thought was her sister nodded. "All right." She turned to the other girl. "You go ahead, Jenny. I'll see you later."

Jenny gave May a hard look then shrugged and walked on up the street.

"I hope I didn't hurt your friend's feelings."

"Oh, she gets huffy over anything. Besides, she's not a special friend. We just work together. Misery loves company, you could say. What did you want to talk to me about?"

May glanced around. The middle of the street was hardly the place to prove their relationship. "Isn't there somewhere we can go and talk privately?"

April pointed to a sign CAFE down a block. "Guess that place is as good as any."

The place was crowded, but they found an empty booth in the back. Taking the two mugs of coffee they had ordered at the counter, they sat down. The girl from the factory slid the glass sugar container toward her and liberally scooped two heaping spoonfuls into her mug and stirred. "So what makes you think we're related?"

Now, after all this time, the moment had come. May looked at the girl sitting opposite her. Bony wrists protruded from too-short coat sleeves. Her hands were chapped, her fingernails broken. Up close her skin was very pale, and there were shadows like lavender bruises under dark-lashed eyes.

"Well? I thought we came here to talk. So what did you have to tell me?" The sharp question brought May back to the present.

"My name's May. Does that mean anything to you?"

"No, should it?"

"*April* and *May*. They go together, don't you see?"

"No, I don't. Just because your name's May and mine's April don't mean anything that I can see."

"They're not what you would call usual names."

The other girl's expression remained blank. "I don't know who named me. Like Jenny said, I grew up in an orphanage."

"Not your whole life, April." May paused and then asked, "Didn't you live in Penfield, Arkansas? With the Barstows?"

The other girl's face flushed then turned pale. She started to say something but began to cough and had to take a sip of her coffee.

"We were both put on the Orphan Train and placed out in different homes." In a rush May told April the entire story. "It's all in this." May pulled the manila folder in which she had placed the newspaper account of the Orphan Train coming to Emeryville, along with the picture of the two little girls. She tapped her finger on the picture. "That's us. You and me. May and April." She laid the folder between them on the table. May tapped her index finger on the cover. "You can read it all for yourself. I believe we're sisters."

April made no move to pick up the folder. Instead, she stared at May silently. The cash register rang. At the next table a couple sat down. May continued to wait for April to react. She leaned forward. "I've been trying to find you for months, tracking down every possibility." She paused another few seconds, then in a low, intense voice she said, "I know who our real parents are. I have their names."

"Some kind of parents. Dumped us."

"I don't think it was our mother's choice. I think she was desperate."

"What makes you so sure?"

"I've seen the beautiful little outfits we were dressed in—smocked dresses, ruffled bonnets. We weren't neglected."

There was no comment.

"I know who our real father is too, April," May rushed on. "He's a musician, a well-known one in Boston. Sebastian Revoc."

"Who cares? He certainly must not have cared about us." A cough interrupted whatever else she might have said.

"That cough sounds terrible. Have you been to a doctor?"

"No, I have some medicine I'm taking for it."

May tried again, "Please listen, I am telling you the truth. I want you to come back with me to Boston. We can search some more, maybe find our mother, if she is still alive. Maybe together we can contact our father."

The other girl looked uncomfortable. "What good would that do?" Then she added sarcastically, "Unless he's a millionaire and we've inherited a fortune."

May took a long breath. "That's another thing, April. My adopted parents are dead. So is my aunt. They left everything to me. It's certainly not a million dollars, but there's enough to give us a small income for the rest of our lives."

April's eyes widened. "You must be crazy to come here and tell this story to a perfect stranger and offer her a share of your inheritance."

"It's not crazy, and you're not a stranger. You're my sister. I'm sure of it. And it's only fair," May said.

The other girl finished her coffee and stood up.

"I don't know what your game is, but I'm not playing it. I've got to go." She stood, picked up her check, and started walking to the cash register.

"Wait, please. Won't you even take this folder with you, read it?" May pleaded, following her. "Please."

"Oh, all right." Reluctantly April took the folder.

"And after you do, can we meet again to talk some more?"

April hesitated.

"If you're not convinced, I won't bother you anymore."

"How long will you be in town?"

"I'll stay as long as it takes."

April lifted her eyebrows. "All right. Sunday's my day off. The town park. One o'clock."

"Fine," May agreed.

They walked out into the chilly evening. The chimney stacks of the factory were filling the air with acrid smoke.

April tucked the folder under her arm, plunged her hands into her coat pockets, and started walking in the opposite direction.

May watched the thin, shabby figure walk down the street and disappear around the corner. Her heart ached. She had expected the other girl to be happy at the information she had given her. She had imagined a joyous reunion. Instead, it had been one of grudging consent even to listen. Obviously she was suspicious that any of this could be the truth.

May couldn't blame her for being cautious. In fact, she understood. She too had been stunned by the report in the newspaper article about the children on the Orphan Train, and she had also found it difficult to believe she was one of them.

April had lost two mothers. Maybe that kind of wound never healed, maybe it was a loss that lasted forever. Was April too emotionally damaged, too hardened to be receptive to the truth?

May prayed that wasn't the case. She hoped that somehow the article in the folder would trigger April's memories and all that May had told her would make sense.

An icy blade of wind knifed through May. She shivered, turned, and headed toward the dingy hotel. This was Thursday. She had three days to wait before meeting April again. By that time maybe April would have recovered from the shock and accepted the truth that they were long-lost sisters. But May wasn't sure that would happen.

Back in her tiny room in the boardinghouse, April lifted the glass chimney of the oil lamp, tested the wick, then lit it. A pale circle of light illuminated the small table and folder May had given her.

As she read the yellowed newspaper clipping over and over, a kind of vague conviction gripped her. There was no denying such a thing as the Orphan Train had really existed. But had she been among the children brought to Emeryville and placed out there?

Of course, she remembered the Barstows—that was the happiest time of her life. But before that? She couldn't remember.

"Orphaned and abandoned" the newspaper account said. "Dumped" was the harsher expression her fellow orphans had used at the County Orphanage.

April pressed her fingers against her now throbbing temples, squeezed her eyes shut, and tried to remember. Thoughts came in pieces—a cold, frightening place, a moist, little hand clinging to hers, a small, shivering body huddled beside her on a hard seat, a rattling sound, a swaying sensation of . . . a train? A voice repeating inside her head, "Take care of your baby sister." Was that real or just her imagination, an idea brought on by a strange encounter with a young woman she had never seen before? She didn't know. All she knew was that she felt confused, deeply troubled.

What was she supposed to do next?

17

On Sunday May waited anxiously for April. She felt immense relief when she saw her coming. As she approached, May noticed again how thin she was.

"Oh, I'm so glad to see you. I was afraid you might not come," May said.

"I had your stuff, remember?" April replied shortly. She pulled the folder out and handed it back to May.

"That's right. So what do you think?"

April coughed hoarsely before answering. "It could be."

"Let's sit down so we can talk about it," May suggested, gesturing toward one of the park benches. "Do you believe what I told you?"

"Like I said, I've never worried that much about my background. Just got along the best I could."

"But do you remember being on a train or having a little sister?" May leaned forward eagerly.

"I remember the Barstows. But a lot has happened to me since then . . ." She gave a little shudder. "A lot of it not so good." She shrugged. "What good does that do? You can't change anything."

"But that's just it, we *can* change things. Now that we've found each other, everything's different. Can't you see that?"

"What's to be gained? I've got my life, you've got your's. Haven't you?" She regarded May sharply. "I didn't ask, but are you married?"

"No, but I'm engaged to a wonderful man. He'll be so happy to know I found you. We've put off our wedding several times because—"

Just then, April had a fit of coughing. Concerned, May broke off what she was saying. "You've still got that awful cough. You really should see a doctor."

April pulled out a handkerchief and wiped her mouth. May took the opportunity to plead, "April, why don't you come to Boston with me. We can search some more, maybe find our mother, maybe try again to contact our father."

"Just like that, huh?"

"I'll pay for the train tickets, the hotel. I told you, I have enough money for both of us."

April gave her a withering glance. "Oh, sure."

"It's true, April. I want you to share whatever I have."

April stood up. "You don't get it, do you?" she demanded. "I've got a job. I can't just up and quit." She shook her head. "I guess you can't help it." She cast a glance that was half pity, half contempt at May. "Well, I guess I'll be getting along." Her words had a finality about them that sent a sliver of fear through May.

"But you can't just leave it like this, not when we've just found each other. Please think about coming to Boston with me." Afraid April was going to walk away, walk out of her life again, May jumped up and quickly said, "I'll stay over, give you time to think about it. If you change your mind, contact me at the hotel. May I have your address?"

"I live in a boardinghouse the mill owns. Most of my chums live there too. 1230 Bedloe Street." April paused to cough.

"You will think about all this, won't you?" May persisted.

April started toward the park gate then suddenly stopped and turned to look at May—a long, penetrating look. Then she asked, "Didn't nothing bad ever happen to you just because you were an orphan?"

May was taken aback. For a minute her mind went blank. Without waiting for an answer, April walked away. "Take care of yourself," May called after her, but April did not turn around or wave.

May felt disheartened. Her hopes for a joyous reunion had been shattered. April distrusted her, suspected her motives. No wonder. Maybe May was asking too much. As April had pointed out, she had appeared out of nowhere, told this fantastic story, asked April to accept and believe it. May couldn't blame her for not believing it, but what more could she do to convince her?

With a sigh, May sat back down on the bench. April's question lingered hauntingly. Then suddenly with cold certainty a memory returned. Kindergarten, Betty Sue's birthday party, May the only one not invited, and

Miranda's explanation: "It's because you're an orphan."
May felt weak with remembered hurt. The tears, the
breathlessness as she ran home to tell her mother.
"Miranda says I'm an orphan! I'm not, am I?"

But the long withheld truth was that she *was* an
orphan. She was only just now beginning to understand
what that meant. Was that the reason her parents had
pulled up stakes and moved to Cedar Falls? It all made
sense now. May began to cry. Maybe there had been
other times she didn't remember. She had been so surrounded by protective love. But this one was painful
enough. She was glad April had asked that question. It
went to the very heart of what separated them and what
they had in common. Couldn't April see that?

May felt overcome with emotion. Slowly she walked
back to the hotel. She picked up her key at the desk,
went upstairs, and let herself into the room. She sat
down on the edge of the bed without taking off her hat
or coat and stared at the wall. She had done all she
could. What happened next was out of her hands. It was
up to April now.

Had all this been an impossible journey? A futile
effort? No. May refused to believe that. She had come
too far to give up now. No matter what.

Praying was natural to May. She had been brought
up to do so in times of both need and thanksgiving. She
remembered a poem by the famous poet Tennyson she
had memorized in high school. "More things are wrought
by prayer than this world dreams of." Was it true? Had
their frightened, young mother's prayers brought her

two daughters together at last? Surely, they had been heard and answered.

May slipped to her knees, lowered her head into her hands, and prayed earnestly, "Let April come to believe I am her sister."

Two more days dragged by with no word from April. May knew she had to try one more time to convince April to go to Boston with her. She was at the factory gate when the early shift ended. She saw April's fellow worker Jenny, but April was not with her. May pushed through the crowd and grabbed Jenny's arm. "Where is April?"

"What's that to you?" Jenny demanded.

"I wanted to see her again before I left town."

"Yeah? Well, she's sick. She just worked half day Monday, nearly passed out. Two of us had to take her back to her room." Jenny jerked her head back toward the factory. "They docked her pay but not us for taking her."

"How sick is she? I know she had a terrible cough. Has she seen a doctor?"

"A doctor?" Jenny sneered. "Doctors don't come cheap." She looked May over from head to foot, taking in the expensive outfit. "But I guess you wouldn't know about *that*."

May ignored the snide remark. "Will you see her tonight?"

"We live in the same boardinghouse."

"Will you please tell her that May Chandler wants to see her? Ask her if there's anything I can do for her?"

Jenny started to walk away, but May stopped her again.

"Tell her it's really important."

"Sure, I'll tell her."

May spent another sleepless night in the dingy hotel. She woke with a headache but new determination. She had to convince April that they had a common bond she wasn't willing to forget.

A sallow-faced woman with graying red hair twisted into a sloppy topknot answered May's knock at the boardinghouse.

"Does April Barstow live here?"

"She's took to her bed, nasty cough. She's been off work a coupla days. That means no pay. Her rent's due the first of the month so she better get better quick."

May controlled her indignation at the woman's attitude. "May I see her?"

"If you're not scairt of catchin' whatever she's got."

May brushed by the woman into the dark hallway. It smelled of grease and boiled cabbage. At the stairway she turned for directions.

The woman pointed. "She's in the third room on the left at the top."

May went up the stairs and tapped at the door. A weak voice said, "Come in." She walked into a small, bleak room where April lay in a narrow, black iron bed, her tangled hair spread on a gray-sheeted pillow. May was shocked at how sick she looked.

"What are you doing here? I thought you'd be gone by now," April said hoarsely. Whatever else she might have said was cut off by deep, ragged coughing.

May rushed to the washstand, poured a tumbler full of water from the pitcher, and brought it to April. She slipped her arm under her thin shoulders to raise her up and held the glass to her cracked lips.

"April, you can't stay here. You're too ill. We must get you into the hospital where you can be looked after properly." April's protest was broken by another fit of coughing. When it was over, May held up her hand.

"There's no use arguing. I'll see to everything."

May ran downstairs and rapped on the the landlady's door. "We must get April to the hospital at once. Please send someone to get me a cab. I'll take her there."

Looking both shocked and relieved that someone was taking charge of a boarder who might die on her, the woman hurried to follow May's orders.

Within twenty minutes, April was admitted to the hospital, where she was diagnosed with pneumonia. She was not placed in the charity ward, where she might have been had May not paid for a private room. The attending doctor told May, "It's a good thing you acted so promptly bringing her here and getting her emergency treatment."

April remained in an oxygen tent for three days. The day she was able to sit propped up with pillows and take some solid nourishment, May confronted her. "Now, will you listen to sense and come with me so I can take care of you?"

April managed a wan smile. "What else can I do? I've lost my job and my room's probably been rented."

May pretended to be stern. "So, you'll have to come back to Cedar Falls with me and stay until you're completely well."

After a slight delay, April said, "Thanks, May. The doctors say you saved my life."

"If I did, I'm glad." May smiled. "There's an ancient Chinese proverb that says when you save someone's life you're responsible for them forever."

A flicker of amusement brightened April's eyes.

"Leave it to you to come up with a quirky reason like that."

"Well, then it's settled. As soon as you're well enough you'll come to Boston with me and then to Cedar Falls. We'll have a chance to get to know each other, find out what it's like to be sisters."

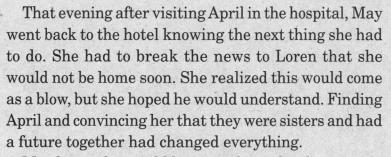

18

That evening after visiting April in the hospital, May went back to the hotel knowing the next thing she had to do. She had to break the news to Loren that she would not be home soon. She realized this would come as a blow, but she hoped he would understand. Finding April and convincing her that they were sisters and had a future together had changed everything.

May knew she would have to phrase her letter carefully, selecting the right words to explain. She took a deep breath and began to write.

My dearest Loren,

I know you will be happy to know that I have at last found my sister. However, she is seriously ill. She is in the hospital recovering from pneumonia. The doctors say only the best of care, nourishing food, and plenty of rest will bring about a full recovery. I have promised to do everything possible to help her regain her health and strength.

In the meantime, we have had several long talks, and I have persuaded her to go to Boston with me as soon as she is well, and together we will trace our parents.

> I realize how difficult this will be for you to accept, but please try to understand how important this is to us.

May lifted her pen from the paper. There was still the final conclusion to write. She wanted to phrase it so that Loren could do nothing but agree. She had to devote herself to helping her sister regain her health and to building a strong, loving relationship between them. That is what Aunt Wilma had wanted her to do. It was what their poor young mother would have wanted for them—to be together at last. She started to write again.

> You have been so patient and understanding about all this from the start, and I know you will continue to be support-ive. I do love you and look forward to the day we can be together—all three of us. I have told April so much about you. I will write to you from Boston and let you know of the progress of our search.
>
> Always,
> May

As soon as the doctors said April was well enough to travel, the two set out for Boston. They took a furnished apartment and continued the search May had begun to find out more about their parents, especially their mother. Finally, after spending several hours in the courthouse going through county records of births and deaths, they were successful. They found Alisa Clarke had died in 1896, just one year after she had put them on the Orphan Train.

"She must have been ill, too sick and poor to take care of us," said April.

"The adoption release I saw on Miss Roth's desk said she was a student. She probably had no way to support two little girls."

April's expression hardened. "That Revoc! He must have been a scoundrel."

"Or maybe just young, irresponsible himself. Musicians don't make a great deal of money."

April didn't reply. She had her own opinion of the man who was their father.

Further checking revealed where their mother was buried. With armloads of flowers, they took the trolley out to the cemetery. They walked along the graveled paths among ornate monuments and elaborate gravestones until they came to a more modest part of the cemetery. There they found a small, gray headstone simply marked "ALISA CLARKE, 1872–1896."

"She was so young," murmured May. "Only nineteen when she had you, April. Twenty when she had me. You have to wonder if she ever knew any happiness."

April's mouth drooped. "She knew loneliness, that's for sure."

Both began to cry unashamedly for the young mother who had loved them so dearly but had to give them up. Abandoned, alone, and ill, what else could she have done?

"At least we're together now," May consoled April as they left the grave site and headed back to the city.

That evening they talked far into the night. April confided her dream of having a little shop some day.

"Oh, April, I want to help you do that!" May exclaimed.

For once April did not dismiss May's generosity. She was discovering what it meant to have someone who really cared about her and wanted the best for her. She was learning what a sister was.

The very next day May wrote to Loren.

Dearest Loren,

April will be coming back to Cedar Falls with me. I know we spoke of using money from the sale of Aunt Wilma's house for a down payment on a house for us when we get married. With your permission I would like to do something else. I want to deed Aunt Wilma's house over to April so that she can start her hat shop without any worries and conduct it from there. She is a talented milliner, very creative. I know that given the chance she can make a success of her business.

19

The following Sunday April and May attended church together. The hymns reminded April of the ones Peg Barstow had taught her and the Bible stories she had read her. During the service April realized she had a great deal for which to thank God. She had not attended church regularly in recent years, but she intended to change that.

Upon returning to the hotel, they bought a newspaper. In it, April found an announcement that seemed to jump out from the page in bold type.

"Look at this, May!" April exclaimed, handing her the section of the paper she was reading.

A boxed advertisement announced "In concert: Sebastian Revoc, recently returned from European tour, will give two benefit concerts for the Music Conservatory of which he is a graduate and master teacher." The date of the first concert was the following Sunday.

The two looked at each other with the same thought.

"Of course, we must go." It meant postponing their trip another week. May wrote Loren, hoping he would understand.

Dearest Loren,

I'm sure you see why we feel we must see our father in person. It will provide us with some answers, we hope. Of course we do not mean to approach him. He has already shown himself to be a person of no conscience. But for our own satisfaction, we do not feel we should pass up this chance.

The day of the concert was cold, the sky overcast with little flurries of snow. May and April did not talk much on the trolley ride to the concert hall where the benefit was to be held.

It was a magnificent building and very imposing. Inside was just as grand with plush carpeting, gilded chandeliers, and velvety cushioned seats.

They bought their tickets and picked up a program in the lobby. Then an usher showed them down the aisle.

"I don't think Revoc is a struggling artist any longer," April whispered to May. "He must be very successful to be playing in this kind of place."

Upon opening their programs they saw a picture of the musician. Posed with his violin tucked under his chin, his bow lifted, his wavy dark hair falling forward on his brow, he was the epitome of the romantic musician. But what about the *real* man? Who was he? Was the man who had fathered them simply a heartless rogue? Were there any justifying reasons for what he had done? Any circumstances to explain his desertion of their young mother?

Suddenly there was a stirring throughout the concert hall. The orchestra members filed in and took their places. Soon came the sound of the various instruments being tuned. Then the conductor entered, went to the podium, bowed to the audience, and accepted the applause that followed. He gestured with his right arm, and the spotlight moved to the wings, where a minute later out walked the feature soloist—Revoc, a tall man in evening clothes, dark hair silvered slightly at his temples. He took a bow, acknowledged the conductor and members of the orchestra. The conductor turned to the orchestra, tapped his baton, and the music began.

The beautiful sound of the violin rose, fell, and swirled through the hall with its magic. May felt sad. It grieved her that this artist had not shared his life, his talent, his love of music with his children.

Beside her April was having a different reaction. She was filled with anger. How could this man have been so cruel? Had he ever been a part of their lives? Ever held them in his arms or looked at them with love? The thought of the young student who had fallen hopelessly in love with him, who had given up everything for him, and who in the end had been abandoned, filled April with rage.

A burst of enthusiastic applause all around her startled April back to the present. Revoc was bowing. Then he shook hands with the conductor and left the stage. People were shouting, "Encore!" but he did not return.

When the concert was over, May and April made their way with the rest of the departing audience into the lobby and outside.

April clutched May's arm. "Let's go around to the back of the building and see if we can catch him leaving."

"But why?" May was feeling shaken by the whole experience. But April was pulling her along with her.

"We'll wait here, see if he comes out."

Shielded from the wind behind a pillar, they waited until a shiny car drove up. A uniformed chauffeur got out and opened the back door just as Revoc, accompanied by a short, stocky man, emerged from the building. Before May could stop her, April darted forward. Waving her program she called in a loud voice, "Mr. Revoc!"

The two men halted, and April ran up to them. "Could I have your autograph?"

Revoc hesitated a moment, then with an air of weary resignation, he took the program and the pen his companion handed him and scribbled his name. He thrust the program back at April. She did not take it immediately but stood there staring directly into his face. Impatiently, Revoc shoved it into her hand, then he and his companion continued down the steps, got into the car, and drove away.

"How did you have the courage to do that?" May gasped.

"I wanted to see if he recognized me at all. We know from his picture we don't look like him, so we must look like our mother. I wanted him to get a good look at me, see if anything about me reminded him of Alisa Clark."

"And?"

April took a long breath. "I could almost testify I saw *something*—a flicker of recognition. Of course I can't be sure. At least I had the satisfaction of trying."

May gave her a hug.

"You're so brave. I wouldn't have dared."

April smiled, remembering Peg Barstow's last words to her long ago. "Be a brave girl, April." Well, she had tried to be.

That night in a letter to Loren, May told him about their encounter with Sebastian Revoc. Then she added,

> We now feel we have fulfilled our goal of finding out about our birth parents and why we were released for adoption. Of course, this is not the entire story, but at least we have unraveled part of the mystery of our past. We have our train reservations for the twentieth, next Thursday, and we shall be in Cedar Falls that Saturday. Will you meet us? I can't wait to see you.
>
> Love always,
May

Anyone seeing them at the train station could not mistake that they were sisters, maybe even twins.

As they stood there amid the noise and bustle, the hurrying people, the porters and red caps, the rattling of luggage carts on the cement platform, something happened. They looked at each other. There was something so familiar about it all. For a moment they were both caught up in a moment of remembrance.

Suddenly May was thrust back in time. Vividly, the feeling came of being small, helpless, carried away sobbing against a man's broad shoulder, reaching back with her arms to a forlorn little figure waving one tiny hand to her, calling frantically a name.

"Cissy," May said through stiff lips, at first in a whisper, then outloud. "Cissy. *Cissy?*"

A strange expression passed over April's face. A glimmer of recognition came into her eyes, followed by tears. She took a step forward, and the two embraced.

May felt as though her heart were breaking, then it was filled with a soaring happiness. April remembered. And now so did she. The years—all the lost yesterdays—faded away, and May knew it was not an ending but a new beginning. Two sisters, lost to each other for so long, were at last reunited.

About the Author

I grew up in a small Southern town, in a home of story-tellers and readers, where authors were admired and books were treasured and discussed. When I was nine years old, an accident confined me to bed. As my body healed, I spent hours at a time making up stories for my paper dolls to act out. That is when I began to write stories.

As a young woman, three books had an enormous impact on me: *Magnificent Obsession, The Robe,* and *Christy.* From these novels I learned that stories held the possibility of changing lives. I wanted to learn to write books with unforgettable characters who faced choices and challenges and were so real that they lingered in readers' minds long after they finished the book.

The Orphan Train West series is especially dear to my heart. I first heard about these orphans when I read an *American Heritage* magazine story titled "The Children's Migration." The article told of the orphan trains taking more than 250,000 abandoned children cross country to be placed in rural homes. I knew I had to write some of their stories. Toddy, Laurel, Kit, Ivy and Allison, and April and May are all special to me. I hope you will grow to love them as much as I do.

Jane Peart lives in Fortuna, California, with her husband, Ray.

Orphan Train Heritage Society of America

We are an organization of 430 members, mostly descendants of actual Orphan Train Riders. We enjoy purchasing and giving Jane's books to our children and grandchildren. We can rest assured that Jane's books will always be suitable for our readers. We appreciate her style of writing and her treatment of the way society looked upon the Riders. She lets them retain their pride and dignity as they work through the various traumas that fill their young lives.

Today's foster children read Jane's books and quickly relate to Toddy, Laurel, Kit, Ivy, and Allison. Hopefully the series will continue. The Orphan Train Riders live on.

Sincerely,
Mary Ellen Johnson,
Founder and Director

The Orphan Train West for Young Adults Series

They seek love with new families . . . and turn to God to find ultimate happiness.

The Orphan Train West for Young Adults series provides a glimpse into a fascinating and little-known chapter of American history. Based on the actual history of hundreds of orphans brought by train to be adopted by families in America's heartland, this delightful series will capture your heart and imagination.

Popular author Jane Peart brings the past to life with these heartwarming novels set at the turn of the century, which trace the lives of courageous young girls who are searching for fresh beginnings and loving families. As the girls search for their purpose in life, they find strength in God's unconditional love.

Follow the girls' stories as they pursue their dreams, find love, grow in their faith, and move beyond the sorrows of the past.

Look for the other books in the Orphan Train West for Young Adults series!

Left at Boston's Greystone Orphanage by her actress mother, exuberant Toddy sets out on the Orphan Train along with her two friends, Kit and Laurel. On the way, the three make a pact to stay "forever friends." When they reach the town of Meadowridge, Toddy joins the household of Olivia Hale, a wealthy widow who wants a companion for her delicate granddaughter, Helene. Before long, Toddy wins their hearts and brightens their home with her optimism and zest for life.

As the years pass, Toddy brings much joy to Helene and Mrs. Hale. Yet happiness eludes her. Is Toddy's yearning for a home only a dream?

LAUREL

JANE PEART

Laurel

Orphan Train West
SERIES

Shy, sensitive Laurel is placed at Boston's Greystone Orphanage when her mother enters a sanitarium. After her mother's death, Laurel is placed on the Orphan Train with Kit and Toddy, destined for the town of Meadowridge. There she is adopted by Dr. and Mrs. Woodward, who still grieve for the daughter they lost two years earlier.

Laurel brings a breath of fresh air— and much love—into the Woodwards' home. As she grows up, though, Laurel longs to discover her true identity. Her search leads her to Boston, where she uncovers secrets from her past. But will Laurel's new life come between her and the love she desires?

KIT

After her grieving, widowed father leaves Kit, her younger brother, and her baby sister at Greystone Orphanage in Boston, Kit wants desperately to bring the family back together. But the younger children are adopted and Kit is sent West on the Orphan Train. Along the way, she and her friends, Toddy and Laurel, make a pact to be "forever friends." At the end of their journey, they each go to live with different families in the town of Meadowridge.

Kit is taken by the Hansens, a farm family who wants to adopt a girl to help the weary mother of five boys. Kit rises above her dreary situation by excelling in her schoolwork. But will she ever realize her secret longings to love and be loved?

IVY & ALLISON

Ivy Austin dreams about being adopted and leaving the orphanage, but when her life takes a strange turn, she ends up on the Orphan Train. There she meets Allison, whose pretty features and charm are sure to win her a new home. Worried that she will be overlooked by potential parents and not wanting to be left behind, Ivy acts impulsively.

As Ivy and Allison grow up together in the town of Brookdale, their past as insecure orphans still hurts, even though they have loving adoptive families. Their special friendship is a comfort, but is it strong enough to withstand the truth of Ivy's secret?